"Your hair," El[...] "What color is you[...]

Despite the fact that her voice sounded far too needy in her own ears, she had to know the entire picture. She had to *see* him.

"Dark brown."

Like molasses. Like his voice.

"Your eyes?"

"Dark brown."

She fought the burgeoning awareness filtering through her veins, filling her with a languid heat. It wasn't right to be responding this way to a volunteer. It wasn't in the least bit businesslike.

But, dear heaven above, she was beginning to form an image of him in her head, which wouldn't go away. The clarity of her imagination was strange and disturbing, as if somewhere, somehow, she'd seen him before....

Dear Reader,

Welcome to another joy-filled month of heart, home and happiness from Harlequin American Romance! We're pleased to bring you four new stories filled with people you'll always remember and romance you'll never forget.

We've got more excitement for you this month as MAITLAND MATERNITY continues with Jacqueline Diamond's *I Do! I Do!* An elusive bachelor marries a lovely nurse for the sake of his twin nieces—will love turn their house into a home? Watch for twelve new books in this heartwarming series, starting next month from Harlequin Books!

How does a proper preacher's daughter tame the wildest man in the county? With a little help from a few Montana matchmakers determined to repopulate their town! Sparks are sure to fly in *The Playboy's Own Miss Prim*, the latest BACHELORS OF SHOTGUN RIDGE story by Mindy Neff!

An expectant mother, blinded from an accident, learns that the heart recognizes what the eye cannot see in Lisa Bingham's touching novel *Man Behind the Voice*. And when a little boy refuses to leave his ranch home, his mother must make a deal with the brooding, sexy new owner. Don't miss Carol Grace's delightful *Family Tree*.

Spice up your summer days with the best of Harlequin American Romance!

Warm wishes,

Melissa Jeglinski
Associate Senior Editor

Man Behind the Voice

LISA BINGHAM

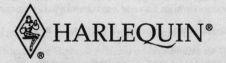

HARLEQUIN®

TORONTO • NEW YORK • LONDON
AMSTERDAM • PARIS • SYDNEY • HAMBURG
STOCKHOLM • ATHENS • TOKYO • MILAN • MADRID
PRAGUE • WARSAW • BUDAPEST • AUCKLAND

To Danilyn.
Thank you for teaching me to see with new eyes.

ISBN 0-373-16835-7

MAN BEHIND THE VOICE

Copyright © 2000 by Lisa Bingham.

Visit us at www.eHarlequin.com

Printed in U.S.A.

ABOUT THE AUTHOR

Lisa Bingham is a resident of Tremonton, Utah—a rural farming community where the sounds of birds and the rustle of wheat can still be heard on hot summer evenings. She has written both historical and contemporary romances and loves spending time watching her characters grow. When she isn't writing, she spends time with her husband on his three-hundred-acre farm and teaches English at a local middle school.

Books by Lisa Bingham

HARLEQUIN AMERICAN ROMANCE

HARLEQUIN INTRIGUE

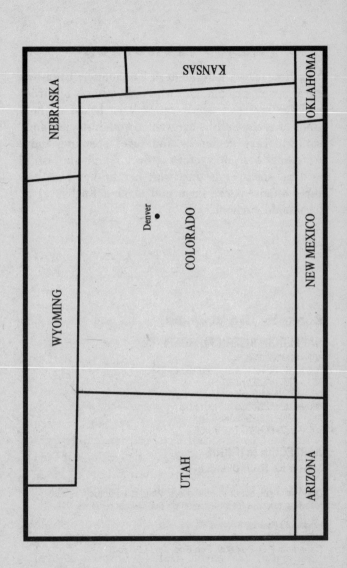

Prologue

Jackson MacAllister groaned, his body pounding with a thousand aches, the worst of which seeming to center over his left eye. Inexplicably, his mind stumbled through a dense emotional fog, while his eyes stared at...

At what?

It took several long moments for Jack to realize that his face had been pressed into something soft. A balloon?

No.

An airbag.

In a sickening rush, he was inundated with memories. For most of the day, the weather had been cold, with the windchill factor causing temperatures to drop to well below freezing. Jack, who had been working with a filming crew near Estes Park, Colorado, had been eager to finish his assignment and begin the long drive to California.

With the road ahead of him and weeks of difficult stunt work behind him, Jack had been making good time out of the canyon. Traffic was sparse at eight in the evening. The weather had long since chased most of the skiers away.

Jack had been whistling softly to himself, enjoying the hot coffee he'd taken with him from the commissary and the soft music drifting from the speakers of his brand-new pickup truck. But then, Jack had topped the rise and taken a blind curve.

As soon as he focused on the scene awaiting him in the valley below, his good mood vanished. Silhouetted in the headlights of another car, he saw a three-car accident blocking the road in front of him.

Immediately, Jack's instincts kicked in. Years of stunt driving for films made his actions second nature. He'd swiftly applied the truck's antilock brakes, steering well away from the accident should he overshoot his mark. But just when he'd begun to believe he had the situation under control, the truck hit a patch of black ice and...

Jack winced, remembering the horrible screech of metal, the exploding whoosh of his air bag, the grinding explosive sound of his car colliding with the others. And then a scream.

A scream.

In an instant, his mind cleared and Jack was suddenly galvanized into action. Ignoring the aches and pains of his own body, he grappled with his door handle, all to no avail. The impact had dented the panel to a point where nothing short of the "Jaws of Life" would open it.

Reaching behind the bench seats of his pickup, he grasped a toolbox. Flinging open the lid, he removed a small metal awl. By placing the tip against the window and applying pressure...

Bam!

The pane shattered, spraying him with tiny chunks of glass. Tucking the awl and a small first-aid kit into the deep pocket of his jacket, Jack carefully slid through the aperture, assessing the scene that lay before him.

A delivery truck was evidently the first vehicle to hit the ice, skidding sideways across the road so that it was hit in turn by a large sedan, and then a smaller compact car.

Jack's heart thudded painfully in his ears as he saw the damage his much larger vehicle had made to the tiny car. "Donormobiles" One-Eye Sullivan, Jack's co-worker and friend, called the small compact cars. The diminutive vehicles were great on gas mileage and kind to the wallet, but in a high-impact crash they provided only a minor buffer between the driver and an oncoming car.

"Is everybody all right?" Jack shouted to a pair of figures who were beginning to emerge from the sedan.

"I think so," an elderly gentleman called back.

Glancing behind him at the hill to ensure no other cars were about to hurtle toward them, Jack made a sweeping wave to the couple. "Get off the road and away from oncoming traffic."

"What about the other drivers?"

"I'll see what I can do. I need you to watch out for oncoming traffic and let me know me if you see any headlights approaching. That's about the only warning we'll get.''

''I'll whistle at the first sign,'' the white-haired gentleman said as he took his wife's arm and hurried her toward the side of the road. ''Come on, Martha. There's a good girl. We'll climb those rocks there so we'll be out of the way.''

A movement from the direction of the delivery truck caught Jack's attention.

''Are you all right?'' he shouted to the driver.

The man was awkwardly cradling his arm against his chest, and even in the gleam of the headlights, he looked abnormally pale. Jack would bet the man had broken something during impact.

''Fine. Just a...bump.'' He climbed from the driver's seat and jumped to the ground, hissing in pain. In his good hand, he held a set of reflectors and a dozen flares. ''I'll just go mark the road to warn off any approaching cars. I've...'' he sucked in his breath for a moment, waited, then continued ''...I've called dispatch and...911. We should have some help here shortly. Go ahead and check that little car. I thought I heard...a scream.''

With a hiss, the first flare was lit, flooding the wreckage with a macabre reddish glow.

Movingly gingerly, Jack managed to crawl over the twisted wreckage of the compact car. To his horror, the wind shifted at that moment, bringing with it the overpowering scent of gasoline. Too late, Jack saw that a puddle of the liquid was forming beneath the mangled vehicle.

He opened his mouth to call to the driver, but the

man was already halfway up the hill and there was no time to waste.

Scrambling to the far side of the car, Jack peered into the interior. The driver was slumped over the wheel, her long hair spilling around her shoulders. It was obvious from the condition of her own door that she had been attempting to get out of her car when Jack's truck had veered out of control. If Jack had plowed into her a few seconds later...

Not wanting to think of the possibility, Jack rapped sharply on the passenger window.

To his relief, the woman moved, turning to gaze at him with wide-eyed confusion.

"I've got to get you out of there. Now. Are you pinned down in any way?"

She shook her head, then winced, gingerly touching her forehead where blood was pouring from a gash next to her hairline.

Jack yanked on the passenger door handle, to no avail.

"Cover your face with your arms. I'm going to break the window."

As soon as she'd done as he asked, Jack angled his own head away, then pressed the tip of the awl against the window. Again, in a seeming explosion of glass, the window dissolved. Seconds later, he was reaching through to the woman in the car.

"Can you crawl out? Your gas tank is leaking and I'd feel safer if we could get you out of there as soon as possible."

A wave of panic raced over her features, and as she stared at him wide-eyed, Jack noted that one of her deep blue eyes was slightly more dilated than the other. To a man who surrounded himself with carefully staged "accidents" as a living, he knew that it was a bad sign. Head injury.

"N-no. I've just got a bump."

"Careful, then. We don't know if you've injured your neck."

"No. It doesn't hurt." She rolled as if to demonstrate. "It's just my head. I banged it on the window frame."

Inching onto her knees, she crawled over the gearshift. As soon as he was able to reach her, Jack slipped his hands beneath her arms to support her and gently lifted her from the car. But when she stumbled as he tried to set her upright, he swung her into his arms and held her against him like a child.

Her body was slight and slim, offering him no resistance—a fact that frightened him even more. She had tucked her head into the hollow of his neck. Against his own, her skin felt cool and clammy. He could see the color leeching from her face and knew she was going into shock.

Hurrying as quickly as he dared, Jack carried her well away from the scene of the accident. Laying her on a patch of bare, frozen grass, he ripped off his coat. After taking the first-aid kit from his pocket, he wadded the heavy down jacket into a ball and wedged it under her feet, elevating her legs as much as possible. Then, dragging his heavy sweater over his head, he knelt beside her, draping the wool over her torso.

"Y-you'll be cold," she whispered, her teeth already chattering from shock and the chill of the wind.

He shrugged, doing his best to pretend that wearing little more than a T-shirt in the gusting wind was no big deal.

"I'm fine. Right now, I'm more worried about you, Miss..."

She licked her lips, squinting up at him in the darkness. "Eleanor. Eleanor Rappaport."

"Well, Eleanor. How's the head?"

"Hurts." She squeezed her eyes shut, blinked then opened them again. "I must have banged it on the side of the car when I tried to get out." She frowned. "But then, I already told you that, didn't I?"

Jack felt a twinge of guilt, knowing that it was because of his truck slamming into her that she'd been injured at all.

"Does anything else hurt?"

She shook her head. "I'm really...fine. Don't know why...I feel so...shaky."

He took her hand, squeezing it. "Don't you worry. You've got a nasty goose egg beginning to swell over one eye. You're bound to be a little woozy."

Releasing her hand for just a moment, Jack tore open the first aid kit. Selecting a pre-moistened towelette, he swabbed the gash. To his relief he found that it probably wouldn't require stitches.

Working as quickly as he could, he cleaned the area, then applied a thick gauze bandage. Then he touched her forehead again. She was cold. Cold, clammy and so very, very pale.

Her eyes suddenly opened. She blinked, squeezed them shut for a moment, then peered at him again.

"So blurry."

Jack felt his mouth grow dry. "You can't see?"

"I'm having trouble...focusing...on things."

Since the fact evidently agitated her, he touched her cheek, then took her hand.

"Don't worry about it. You've probably got a concussion or something. A little rest and you'll be fine."

"You never..." she murmured, her voice faint and somehow fragile "...told me...*your* name."

He squeezed her fingers. "Jackson. Jackson Mac—" He broke off, his head lifting. From far away he heard the faint wail of sirens.

"Hear that?" he said. "They've already sent someone to help. In no time at all, you'll be safe and snug inside an ambulance."

But when he searched her face for a sign of relief, he saw instead that she was gazing at him wide-eyed, a look of sheer horror spreading over her features.

"Jackson? Jackson!"

"Shhh," he offered gently, calmly, even as his heart thudded in his ears and the wailing of the sirens grew louder and louder, scraping nerves already raw from the night's events.

"I'm here, Eleanor," he said, wondering if she were about to lose consciousness. Instead, as he bent low, he realized that her eyes were open, but they weren't tracking him. She stared at him blankly, huge tears beginning to well up and spill down her cheeks.

"Jackson, I can't see," she cried, softly at first, then louder, the sobs tearing at his heart. "Jackson! I can't *see!*"

Chapter One

Six Months Later

Jackson MacAllister bolted upright in bed, his own shout echoing in the darkness of the hotel room.

Breathing heavily, he dragged his fingers through his hair, trying to calm the fierce pounding of his head.

The dream. It had come again—as it always did when he was tired or feeling under the weather.

Or recovering from a nasty concussion.

Wincing, Jack swung his legs over the edge of the bed and turned on the bedside lamp. His body throbbed with the aftereffects of injuries he'd sustained on the job that day and the dregs of his dreams, causing his head to ache until he thought his skull would split with the pressure.

Standing, he padded into the bathroom. Under the harsh glare of the overhead light, he shook four aspirin from the bottle on the counter, then gulped them down with a glass of water from the tap.

Only then did he begin to relax.

Willing himself not to think of the dream or the woman who had seemed so real, so vulnerable, he moved to the windows. Pulling the heavy curtains aside, he peered down at the pre-dawn glow seeping over the Lincoln Memorial in the distance.

It had been nearly a week since the stunt car he'd been driving had flipped end-over-end during a staged high-speed chase for the film adaptation of the bestselling techno-thriller ...*Savage Justice*. The scene had been choreographed and reshot three times in the first month of production, but since the director had spent only a quarter of a million dollars more than his budget had allotted, he'd decided to celebrate his good fortune by spending another fifty grand expanding the final chase scene.

Jack grimaced at the irony of the whole situation. Naturally, the director had decided that the footing showing Jack's accident was ''mar-r-r-velous''—as if Jack had planned to roll out of control and finish the take upside down next to a broken water hydrant. If Jack hadn't immediately been rushed to the hospital, he would have grabbed the director by the collar, pinned him against a wall and chastised the man for moving a camera crew into the middle of the road—unannounced. As it was, Jack had still been in the emergency room when he'd received the news that the filming was finally—*finally*—over.

His anger at the director hadn't eased with the announcement. If anything, Jack's ire had increased—to the point where he'd made an effort to ignore the man so that he wouldn't say anything politically incorrect. Jon Palermo might be an idiot, but his films were spectacular, and Jack enjoyed the creative freedom and lucrative budgets that came with a spot on Palermo's crew. In the meantime, he planned to avoid Palermo.

Which was why Jack was booked on the next afternoon flight to Los Angeles. Once he'd returned to California he could put this whole miserable week behind him.

As if of its own volition, his mind quickly strayed away from all thoughts of Palermo to the nightmare that had awakened him.

Eleanor Rappaport. Why did the memories of that night, that woman, still continue to haunt him?

But even as he asked himself the question, he already knew. In the months since the accident, Jack had thought about Eleanor more than he would care to admit. He couldn't seem to banish the image of her lying next to him, gripping his hand, and crying, "I can't see!"

Again, the words shuddered through him like an icy finger touching his heart. He often found himself wondering what had happened in the intervening months. And if she'd ever regained her sight...

He shook his head as if to clear it of his thoughts, then regretted the action when a slicing pain shot through his head.

The time had come to put the memories of that night behind him, he told himself fiercely. After all, Eleanor Rappaport was a stranger to him. Other than those few minutes at the scene of the accident, he had never seen her again.

But he'd tried, a little voice reminded him. He'd

brought a huge bouquet of daisies to the hospital where Eleanor had been taken, only to discover she'd been transferred to another facility.

Sighing, Jack stared out at the jewel-like glow of the historic buildings clustered around the glassy reflecting pool. Maybe the pressures of the job were to blame, but lately the dreams of that night plagued him even more. The details seemed sharper and Eleanor's panic seemed that much more real.

If only he could assure himself that she was all right. If only he knew if she'd regained her sight. If he could see her one more time...

No. He couldn't even think such a thing. She was a stranger to him. And those few moments they'd had together didn't give him the right to interfere.

But she wouldn't have to know.

The moment the thought raced through his head, he tried to push it aside, but it returned with even more force.

If he could somehow find her, he could tell at a glance if she was happy, healthy...

And whether or not she could see.

Again, he tried to bury the idea. He was out of his mind to even consider such a thing.

But he had the time.

And he needed to know.

Already he found himself making plans. Denver. If he could change his flight to Denver, he could—

No!

Again every logical bone Jack possessed insisted that he stop and think about the repercussions of such an action. Eleanor Rappaport was a stranger.

He had no business barging into her life unannounced.

But another part of him, one that reacted on instinct, had taken control of his body. He was filled with impatience, a sudden *hunger* to see her again.

Numbly he turned, making his way to the closet. Slowly at first, then with greater urgency, he began throwing his belongings in his suitcase, banging drawers as he went.

"Hey! Where are you going?"

The door to the adjoining room squeaked open and a stoop-shouldered man glared at Jack.

Jack grimaced, realizing too late that he'd been making enough noise to wake Ira Sullivan, a fellow stuntman and mentor—known to his friends as One-Eye because of the patch he wore over his left eye, the result of a stunt-related accident that occurred years earlier.

"Denver!"

"Denver?" the man echoed incredulously. "What the hell for? I thought we were taking a four o'clock flight to L.A."

"I've got to see someone there."

"Who?"

"Eleanor Rappaport."

One-Eye's mouth gaped. He'd heard all about the accident and was clearly flabbergasted that Jack intended to see Eleanor again. He opened his mouth intending to argue, then closed it again.

"I'll just gather my things. Heaven only knows what kind of trouble you could get into with that

concussion. 'Pears to me you're going to need someone to ride shotgun with you on this little adventure.''

"THERE YOU GO, Ms. Rappaport.'' The bus driver's
rich-as-chocolate voice was accompanied by the
squeal of brakes and the pungent scent of diesel
fumes. "You be careful on your way home, y'hear?
It'll be slippery out there with all that rain.''

"Thanks, Burt.''

Eleanor awkwardly pushed herself to her feet, automatically smoothing the folds of her jumper over
the protrusion of her stomach.

Two months. Two more months and she wouldn't
have to complete the odd contortion of movements
it took to wriggle out of her seat and stand on a
moving bus.

Finally gaining her balance, Eleanor automatically curled her hand around the iron bar overhead
and made her way to the rear doors, her body leaning backward to adjust to the rocking of the vehicle.

Once she was positioned in front of the exit, she
hooked an elbow around the vertical pole and used
her free hand to unfold the red-tipped cane she'd
slipped into her purse, taking great care not to bump
the strident bicycle bell attached to the handle. Burt
came unglued if she rang it on his bus. Something
to do with the fact that he was an ex-police officer—
go figure.

Looping her wrist through the strap, Eleanor
clasped her coat more tightly around her neck, tap-

ping her toe in an impatient tattoo as she waited for
the city bus to come to a standstill. Not that she had
anything important waiting for her when she arrived
home. She merely hated waste—wasted time,
wasted energy, wasted emotion.

Vainly she tried to shake off the impatience and
frustration that invariably settled under her skin with
bad weather. The smells of exhaust, damp earth and
wet wool hung in the air around her, infiltrating her
consciousness like mustard gas. The noise of rain-
drops splatting against the windows and drumming
to the ground muted the sounds she'd become accustomed to absorbing on her ride home from
work—the snore of Ed Mecham, who would sleep
to the end of the line, the rustle of newspapers, the
chatter of the Selma sisters who rode the number
nine to mass each Wednesday and Friday. Calming
sounds. Ritualistic sounds.

The thump of the doors roused her from her stu-
por, and she descended the steep steps, feeling carefully with her toe before stepping onto the curb.
Once safe and sound, she hit the bicycle bell with
her thumb, a signal to Burt Mescalero that he could
drive on.

Behind her, the engine grumbled and whined, and
a fine spray of water splashed the backs of her legs.
Then she was alone.

Eleanor arched her neck to relieve it of the kink
the muscles had developed after an hour huddled at
the cramped food counter of The Flick Theatre, an
establishment near old Larimer Square that was de-

voted to playing classic movies in their original, wide-screen format.

"Damn those gumdrops," she said to herself, referring to a case of candies that had fallen down the back stairs, spilling cellophane-wrapped packages all over the storeroom floor. Eleanor had spent a half hour on her hands and knees picking them up. If not for that small disaster, she would have been home on one of Burt's earlier runs. But...*c'est la vie,* as her mother would say. Everything happened for a reason.

Absolutely *everything.*

A sharp gust of cold air swirled around her ankles, and she huddled even tighter into the shelter of her coat. It was cold this evening. Too cold for the beginning of May, she decided, as she took three precise steps to the center of the sidewalk, turned right and began to count.

One, two, three, four...

She tapped her cane on the wet pavement ahead of her, seeking out the obstacles her eyes couldn't see. Not clearly, anyhow. Sometimes she experienced hazy patches of gray or muted blotches of light. But for the most part her world was one of darkness. An inescapable darkness that would be her constant companion at least until the baby was born. And then...

She didn't want to think about it. Didn't want to think about the corneal transplant surgery her ophthalmologist had proposed, not knowing whether such an operation would allow her to see as she once had or leave her fumbling in a world of light and shadows.

Sixteen, seventeen, eighteen...

Everyone she knew said Eleanor had adjusted beautifully—her doctor, her mother, her co-workers. But Eleanor wasn't so certain. Oh, she could find her way around town, perform her duties at work and live on her own. But sometimes, on nights like these, when she was angry and tired and out of sorts, she couldn't help thinking that she was a poor sport in God's little game of life. Perhaps if she hadn't relied so heavily upon her sight as an artist, she might not have regarded the loss with such bitterness. She might have been able to "suffer with elegance" as her sister Blythe had once advised her to do.

As it happened, she couldn't seem to resign herself to the fact that her identity had been shattered the moment her head had collided with the window frame of her car. The change in fortunes bothered the hell out of her, burning at the pit of her stomach whenever she allowed herself to think about it.

She'd been a good artist, dammit.

She'd been asked to have a show at the National Gallery.

And a partial return of her sight would never allow her to retain the finesse she'd once mastered.

Twenty-six, twenty-seven, twenty-eight...

Eleanor Rappaport's boot heels rapped sharply against the pavement—and for a moment she thought she heard an accompanying set of footsteps behind her. Automatically she quickened her pace. It annoyed her how some people felt that her being blind was the same as being incompetent. She didn't want help crossing the street, she didn't want anyone leading her home like a stray puppy. She could do it herself.

But as she quickened her step, the sounds behind her increased their speed, echoing her own pace. Thinking whoever was behind her wanted to pass, she stopped and turned.

The noises stopped, as well.

The anger that had been building in her all day raged even hotter. She hated being made to appear a fool, almost as much as she hated being made to appear helpless.

"Who's there?" she called out.

No answer. Only the sputter of the rain gurgling down a nearby gutter.

Eleanor squinted, blinking against the moisture dripping from her hair, down her face, off her dark glasses, hoping to catch a shadow, a shape. But the light was too poor to allow her even the haziest of images.

Shivering, she began to walk again, crossing the quiet street, moving as quickly as she could. She didn't have the patience for such pranks. It was time she arrived home, out of the rain.

But after only a few steps she realized she'd lost count.

Damn.

Damn, damn, *damn*.

Ringing the bell on her cane, she lifted her head calling out, "Minnie! Maude!"

As she waited for a response from her landladies, who were elderly, unmarried and avid game-show fanatics, a tightness closed around her throat and she paused, swallowing hard. For a moment the frustration closed in on her like a shroud. The same frustration that had dogged her since that night when she'd been pulled from the mangled wreckage of her car. While waiting for an ambulance, she'd focused on a stranger's face. The red glow of flares had flickered over dark hair and even darker eyes. Then the colors had grown dim and died completely away, leaving her grasping at the hand of a stranger as she was plunged into nothingness.

Stop it! She didn't want to remember that night. Not tonight.

Ringing the bell more stridently than before, Eleanor shouted, "Minnie—"

"Here, dear," a sweet, old voice interrupted, providing Eleanor with the bearings she needed.

Minnie.

Since Eleanor's grandmother had lived in this neighborhood before she'd died, Minnie and Maude Vanderbilt had been her dearest friends. They'd even been godmothers to Eleanor's mother, and Eleanor had known them both as a child. She pictured Minnie as she'd been then. Short and plump with cotton-candy hair rinsed a pale shade of yellow. She was the perfect foil for her older sister, Maude, who was tall and reed thin and wore an array of different-colored wigs.

"My lands, you're soaked to the skin, child. Maude's not home right now, but I could fix you a cup of tea. *Jeopardy!* is about to start, and you can watch it with me as you dry out."

Eleanor made her way toward the voice, but it was only when she encountered the rough, peeling paint of a picket fence that the tension building inside her breast eased.

Had someone really been following her? Dogging her steps? The hairs at her nape prickled in warning, but there were no sounds to substantiate the suspicion. Nothing that the rain didn't completely obscure.

As soon as her toe touched the bottom step to the brownstone's stoop, she asked, "Minnie, is there anyone behind me on the sidewalk?" Her voice much weaker than she would have wished.

If Minnie thought the request was odd, she didn't say so. Eleanor caught the scent of geraniums as Minnie leaned forward. "No, dear. There's no one there. Let's get you inside."

When Minnie offered her elbow, Eleanor took it, stepping into the vestibule of the old building and shaking the rain from her coat.

Even so, she knew she hadn't imagined anything.

Someone had been out there.

Someone had followed her home.

"How about that tea?" Minnie asked.

Still shaken, Eleanor headed for the stairs.

"Thanks, Minnie, but I think I'll head up to my own apartment. After the day I've had, I'm ready for a long soak in the tub."

"Very well. You call if you need anything."

"Thanks."

But even as she climbed the steps, Eleanor couldn't push away the feeling that she was being watched.

Chapter Two

Jack MacAllister remained in the shadow of a doorway directly across the street, mere yards from where he had first encountered Eleanor Rappaport.

Less than twenty-four hours had elapsed since Jack had decided to see Eleanor. To his surprise, she'd been easy enough to find. A search of the Internet had resulted in his learning she resided in Denver, and a look at the Yellow Pages had revealed an E. Rappaport. After silently debating with himself, Jack had made a quick call…

The moment he'd heard her voice, he'd felt as if someone had kicked him in the stomach. He'd become suddenly tongue-tied—and feeling like an adolescent fool, he'd hung up without saying a word.

Eleanor Rappaport.

His head was pounding, but this time the sensation had nothing to do with a concussion and everything to do with stunned disbelief. He had seen this woman only once before, at the scene of a horrible accident. He had been there to help drag her from her car, he had cradled her head in his lap as he'd waited for the emergency teams to arrive.

He'd been there to watch the light grow dim in her eyes.

Jack's knees became weak, and he sank onto the top step of the small, family owned grocery store. Bowing his head, he took huge gulps of rain-soaked air in an effort to calm his erratic thoughts. Wave upon wave, the nightmares he'd been experiencing for months inundated his senses, but that was nothing compared to what he had just seen in the flesh. The living embodiment of his dreams.

Growling to himself, Jack stood, striding into the rain and into the night. Whatever internal need had dragged him to Denver had been satisfied, and now he was leaving. For good. He'd seen Eleanor Rappaport. She was still blind, but apparently coping.

And pregnant. Very, very pregnant. Why hadn't he known she was pregnant?

A strange, twisting sensation gripped his chest. The accident had occurred six months earlier, so she couldn't have been too far along when she'd lost her sight.

Jack wrenched his thoughts back into line. Eleanor Rappaport's pregnancy was none of his business.

"What's up?" One-Eye asked from the passenger seat of the too-small rental car.

"Nothing."

"Is that the girl?"

"Yeah." His brief reply discouraged any more questions. "I'm ready to head to L.A. now."

"You what?" One-Eye blurted. "But we just got here. We've checked into a hotel, laid out our dainties—"

"We're going home, One-Eye," Jack said sternly.

One-Eye shrugged and settled back in his seat. "Fine. If you don't want to tell me what brought you all the way to Denver—"

Jack remained silent.

"You know that Rappaport woman is nothing but a stranger." One-Eye grimaced. "'Course, you weren't looking at her like a stranger."

Jack shot the older man a scathing look, but his irritation bounced off the man's weathered hide.

One-Eye still looked perplexed at the reason for their impromptu visit to Denver, so Jack offered what he hoped would sound like a logical explanation. "I've been thinking about her lately. I wanted to make sure she was doing all right."

"Uh-huh." But it was clear that One-Eye thought Jack was leaving something out.

"Now that I've had a chance to see her, I'm ready to go home. Do you have any objections?"

One-Eye shook his head. "That's fine by me. But why can't we have a steak and a good night's sleep before we get back on another plane?"

Jack opened his mouth to insist that they leave Denver. Now. But seeing One-Eye's hopeful expression, he relented.

"Fine. I'll book us on a flight tomorrow morning."

One-Eye grinned. "Now you're talking! Let's find us a place to eat."

"COME ALONG, DEAR. We won't take no for an answer."

Eleanor grimaced, realizing that what Maude said was true. Once Minnie and Maude got an idea in their heads, they would move Heaven and Earth to get their own way.

In many ways Eleanor was grateful for her land-ladies' single-minded determinedness. Such resolve had led them to accompany Regina Rappaport to her daughter's hospital room after the accident. While Regina had stayed by Eleanor's bedside, reassuring Eleanor time and again that she hadn't miscarried, Minnie and Maude had searched for the best specialists in the country. These same doctors had treated Eleanor's injuries, allowing her to see some light and shadow and had given her hope for future transplant surgery. As Eleanor had begun to recover more fully, Minnie and Maude had been there to comfort her when her fiancé had abruptly called off their two-year engagement. They'd weathered her moods from rage to despair—to the euphoria she'd experienced when her ultrasound had revealed no evident trauma to the baby. Bit by bit, they'd bullied and cajoled her into rejoining the "real world." The sisters had even offered her their upstairs apartment in Denver so that Eleanor could continue to live on her own and fend for herself. And once the baby was born...well, they had already made plans to be her live-in nannies.

But there were times Eleanor wished Minnie and Maude could be a bit more malleable. Like tonight. After the day she'd had, Eleanor wasn't in the mood to go out to dinner in a crowded restaurant, eat unfamiliar food, and chit-chat with her mother's godmothers.

"Go on. Get dressed. There's a love," Minnie said with a push at Eleanor's shoulders.

Rolling her eyes, Eleanor realized it would be much easier to surrender than fight.

"Just grit your teeth and bear it, little one," she murmured to the tiny life nestled beneath her heart. Then, with a soothing rub of her hand over her stomach to still the sudden flurry of agitated kicks, she plodded to the bedroom.

JACK WAS SURPRISED when One-Eye decided upon an intimate, elegant restaurant located on the ground floor of the Kensington Hotel. The two of them were led to a small room that held only four tables and had been decorated to resemble a Victorian dining hall.

A waiter in a starched white shirt and pleated black trousers, handed them a menu, then went to gather their drinks.

One-Eye clapped his hands together, surveying the list of food. "Hot damn! This is better than any lunch wagon, isn't it?"

Since both of them had spent most of the last three months eating from catering trucks on the set, Jack had to agree. He couldn't remember the last time he'd been able to sit down to a meal without having a thousand work details waiting for his attention.

"So what's your next project?" One-Eye asked.

Jack shrugged. "I've got an action film scheduled for the fall, but I'm thinking of taking some time off until then."

One-Eye nodded sagely. "That sounds like a winning plan. You look like hell."

Jack grimaced. "Thanks a lot."

"No, I mean it. You look like a horse that's been ridden hard and put away without a rubdown—and it's not just the accident. You've been pushing yourself too much these past few years."

The waiter arrived with their drinks and appetizers, preventing Jack from replying. As he gave his order, he glanced at an oval mirror hanging above a marble fireplace.

Did he really look that bad? Granted, he'd been working hard, lately, but after a couple of weeks, he'd be fine.

"Jack, I know you think I'm pestering you," One-Eye continued as soon as the waiter had left. "But I've been worried about you, boy."

Everyone was a boy to One-Eye.

"I've seen this sort of thing happen before in this business. A man gets himself a reputation for being good at his stunts, he takes every job he can, works long hours, forgets about his own needs."

"Needs?" Jack echoed, his eyes drawn to a figure swimming into view in the old mirror.

Long, dark hair. Blue eyes.

His gut tensed in reaction, a chill sweeping

through his body. Eleanor Rappaport? What was she doing here?

"A man's got to have a life outside his job," One-Eye was saying. "Why, I can't remember the last time I even saw you with a woman. It's not natural, I tell you. If you ask me, I think you should..."

One-Eye's advice lapped over Jack like a warm wave, barely registering in his consciousness. Instead, he found himself watching Eleanor Rappaport as she made her way to the table opposite his own.

Sit down, he found himself silently wishing. *Sit down there, facing me.*

As if she'd heard the words being spoken aloud, she hesitated, then made her way to the far side. A tall woman wearing a raven wig held her chair, then gestured for another elderly woman to do the same. Jack immediately recognized the smaller old woman as being an occupant of the brownstone with the shocking-pink door. Eleanor must live with the pair of women.

Jack watched Eleanor fold her cane, then place it in the bag she'd set on the floor. When she straightened, she looked his way, and he averted his eyes—then mocked himself for such an instinctive reaction. She couldn't see him. She couldn't know he was staring at her.

"Are you finished?"

He started when the waiter reached toward his half-eaten salad.

"No. I'm still working on it."

"Of course."

The waiter placed a bowl of thick seafood chowder on the table, then retreated.

"She's a pretty girl," One-eye commented slyly.

Jack glanced at One-Eye, then away.

"Yes. She is."

"Isn't that the same woman you saw earlier?"

Jack forced himself to keep his attention on his plate and eat.

"Yes. That's her."

One-Eye lapsed into silence for a moment, then said, "So is this meeting an accident?"

Jack glared at him. "You picked the restaurant."

The man chewed thoughtfully. "That's right. I did."

One-Eye's suspicions appeared to have been allayed, but Jack wished his own could be so easily put to rest. The fact that Eleanor had come here, to a table mere feet away from his own, was enough to make a pragmatist believe in the powers of Fate.

"The accident was months ago," One-eye remarked after a moment of silence. "What made you start worrying about her again?"

Jack shrugged. "I guess the rollover in Washington reminded me of her. I've been thinking about her ever since."

Thinking?

Obsessing would be a better term. Ever since her image had begun to haunt him, he'd been unable to concentrate on anything else.

"She seems to be getting along well," One-Eye observed.

"Yes. She does."

Tearing his attention away from the woman, Jack forced himself to eat. He even managed to carry on a normal conversation with One-Eye until the two elderly women led Eleanor out the French doors to the lobby beyond, then left her there. Alone. Jack watched as they went to the desk and began conversing with the manager, leaving Eleanor standing near the tufted armchairs.

One-Eye lapsed into silence—an unusual event for him, especially when his belly was full and the coffee was rich and black.

"Why don't you go talk to her?"

Jack jumped as if One-Eye had touched him with a cattle prod. "What?"

"Go talk to her."

He shook his head. "No, I don't think I should."

"Why not?" One-Eye's grin was lazy. "Hell's bells, I don't think I've ever seen you so antsy."

Jack scowled at the man, then realized One-Eye was right. He hadn't tasted any of his food, even though he'd eaten his fill. All of his energies had been directed toward Eleanor Rappaport.

What would it hurt to talk to her?

Jack stood from the table and made his way through the French doors. With each step he damned himself for feeling a need to make contact with the woman. After all, *she'd* been the one to come to this restaurant. *She'd* been the one to inspire this confrontation.

What did he plan to say to her, anyway? Hi, this is Jack MacAllister? Remember me? I'm the one who held you that night you lost your sight? I know it was an accident, but you probably hate me still because it was my truck that struck your car. Nevertheless, I'd like to...

What? What would he like to say or do for this woman?

Jack halted a few feet away from her, inwardly cursing. This whole situation was insane. There was no casual way to force an introduction. He couldn't approach her out of the blue.

Then, as if his doubts had been heard by some unseen force, he watched disbelievingly as the silk scarf she'd draped over one shoulder caught a gust of air from the front door and fluttered to the floor.

"Damn."

He heard her curse under her breath and grinned. My, my, my. Perhaps she wasn't as prim and proper as she appeared to be in her high-buttoned dress and lacy collar.

Picking up the scarf, Jack did his best to ignore the waft of perfume that twined around his senses.

"I believe this is yours," he said to Eleanor.

She didn't start, so he supposed she must have heard his approach.

"Thank you."

She held her hand out, and he laid the scarf there, resisting the urge to stroke it over her palm to see if her skin was as sensitive as it looked.

"My pleasure."

Her head cocked to one side. "I was with a pair of older women and—"

"They're still at the manager's desk. Would you like me to call them over?"

"No. That won't be necessary. I merely thought they would be done with their negotiations by now."

"Negotiations?"

"My landladies are belly dancing enthusiasts. They would like to schedule the banquet room for an upcoming workshop."

Jack shot a glance at the two women who stood by the desk. "Belly dancing?"

Her lips twitched with open amusement. "It's only one of many pastimes they have. They also indulge in social dancing, anthropology and yoga. They even belong to a gun club."

He whistled softly, liking the way that Eleanor's features had brightened with humor. "That sounds interesting."

She shrugged, and the gesture caused the silky fabric of her dress to move against her shoulders. Idly, he wondered what Eleanor Rappaport would do if he touched her there. Just once. Just long enough to assure himself that she was real.

But then his eyes shifted, and he absorbed the folds of fabric draped over her rounded stomach.

She's real, his inner voice assured him wryly. *She's real and she's off-limits.*

So why didn't the reminder of her condition dissuade him from looking at her? He could feel a faint heat seeping into his arm where she stood closest to him. The hint of perfume that had clung to her scarf also clung to her hair. Her skin.

Jack opened his mouth to say something more, something to give him a reason to linger near her

for a moment longer. But when he heard the elderly
women making their goodbyes to the manager, he
knew it was time to go. He'd decided he didn't want
Eleanor's landladies to see him with their charge.
Why such a thing would matter, he didn't know. But
he needed this moment, this meeting, to be between
him and Eleanor, no one else.

"Will you be all right here alone?" He paused,
then couldn't resist adding, "Perhaps I should wait
until your husband returns."

He knew full well that there had been no male
accompanying the women, but he had to know for
sure.

Eleanor's lips twitched in a faint smile. "There is
no husband," she said patting her stomach gently.
"And I'll be fine. Thank you. My companions seem
to be coming back."

"Then I'll be on my way."

He touched her then. He couldn't help it. He had
to lay his hand over her shoulder and squeeze ever
so slightly.

A bolt of white-hot energy shot through his body.
It took all the will he could muster to tear himself
away and walk resolutely into the dining room.

Chapter Three

"Do you mind telling me why we're in such a hurry to get out of Denver?" One-Eye asked as he dropped his duffel bag on the floor and planted his hands on his hips.

"We're not in a rush," Jack reassured him. "I just want to catch the first flight this morning, that's all."

One-Eye snorted. "There's another one leaving in three hours. Why wake us both at the crack of dawn?"

Jack didn't bother to answer the man. After a restless night, haunted by dreams of Eleanor Rappaport, he was in no mood to humor anyone. He wanted to be rid of Denver as soon as possible.

"If you were to ask me," One-Eye continued without urging, "I'd say your recent concussion must have rattled some of your marbles. You're as jumpy as a one-armed man in a boxing ring. You ought to relax, see the sights. We could take in a tour of the Mint or one of the local resorts. There's baseball, or..."

Barely listening to One-Eye's monologue, Jack packed his belongings into a canvas bag and called the airline to confirm their tickets. Then, after ushering One-Eye from the room, he allowed the older man to drive to the airport, all the while enduring his chatter about the sights they would miss.

Once at the airport Jack paid for the car with his credit card, casting glances at the bold digital clock that ticked off the minutes to his flight. He and One-Eye would have to hurry.

Spurred by his thoughts, Jack rushed to the waiting shuttle bus. "Come on, One-Eye, or we'll miss our plane."

"Coming!" One-Eye grumbled, clearly loath to hurry any more than he had already.

Once the bus had dropped them off at the terminal, Jack checked the overhead monitors, then loped in the direction of the underground train, which would take them to the proper boarding gate. With each jarring step, his head pounded more fiercely, and his chest grew tight with something akin to guilt.

But why should he feel guilty? He'd come to Denver, seen Eleanor Rappaport and reassured himself that she was dealing with her blindness. What more could anyone demand of him? He wasn't indebted to her in any way. The accident all those months ago had been just that…an *accident*. Even Eleanor Rappaport's mother had insisted as much, according to the news report Jack had seen the morning after the incident. No charges had ever been filed against any of the people involved, no lawsuits begun.

So he shouldn't feel anything but relief in escaping Colorado.

As he emerged onto concourse B, Jack heard their flight being announced and breathed a sigh of relief. He and One-Eye had arrived in time to board, but were late enough that Jack wouldn't have to sit in the terminal and ponder the strange events that had brought him to this place. Within hours he would be in Los Angeles, back in his apartment, back in his normal routine.

Jack dodged around the other travelers, taking the escalator steps two at a time, while One-Eye trotted after him like a devoted puppy.

As soon as they arrived in Los Angeles, Jack would arrange some time off for himself. After a few weeks of rest and relaxation, he would be fine. He was sure of it. He wouldn't think about Denver. Or Eleanor Rappaport. He wouldn't wonder what could have happened if he'd stayed for one more day….

Stay. Just one more day, something inside him whispered.

No. He couldn't. He needed to get back home.

"Your ticket, sir?"

Too late he realized he'd been standing in front of the check-in counter, staring into space while a pretty airline employee waited to process his boarding pass.

"Your ticket?"

"Sure." He dragged the crumpled documents

from his breast pocket, but as he handed them to the flight attendant, he was suddenly loath to let go. He became abruptly aware of the throbbing of his head and the aches of his weary body.

Funny, but when he'd been talking to Eleanor, he hadn't remembered his injuries. He'd been so involved with her he hadn't given himself another thought.

"Sir?"

Blinking, he stared at the too-pretty face of the flight attendant. But even as he stared at the woman, he found himself struck with a sudden thought. How was Eleanor going to take care of a child? What steps had she taken for the baby's arrival? It was obvious that Eleanor had adjusted to a life alone, but what about the challenges of caring for an infant as well?

"Is something wrong?"

"No, I—"

The throbbing in his head increased. A tight band of worry tightened around his chest.

One-Eye touched his arm in concern. "Jack? What is it? You've gone as white as a sheet."

He shook his head, trying to clear his thoughts. "Nothing, I—"

But he couldn't finish the sentence. If he left, he would always wonder about Eleanor and her baby. Hell, he didn't even know for sure if she was alone. He knew nothing about her other than she lived with two elderly women in an aging brownstone.

So who was the baby's father? Had Eleanor been

abandoned? Had she been abandoned because of her blindness?

Nausea gripped his stomach, and his anxiety increased.

Holding the ticket more firmly, Jack tried to extend it again, but as he did the sickness intensified. The clerk nearly tore it from his fingers, but he barely noticed.

Dammit all to hell, what was happening to him? He had no business insinuating himself in Eleanor Rappaport's life.

The attendant peered at him in concern. "Your friend is right, sir. You do look pale. Are you sure you don't want me to..."

The words flowed around him like thick honey, but Jack couldn't grasp their meaning. Not when he was being flooded with an overwhelming dread. In an instant he knew that if he stepped on that plane, he would be making one of the biggest mistakes in his life.

"Dammit," he whispered to himself.

Go back, a voice whispered inside him. *You have to go back to her.*

"No."

Too late, he realized he'd spoken the word aloud, because both the flight attendant and One-Eye were studying him strangely.

Cursing under his breath, Jack turned and strode in the opposite direction.

"Sir? Your ticket!"

He didn't stop. He didn't pause. Vaguely he heard One-Eye running after him, but all Jack could think

about was that he would have to confront Eleanor
Rappaport again.

Soon.

JACK HAD ORIGINALLY SUPPOSED that once his decision was made, he would grow comfortable with
the thought of seeing Eleanor Rappaport again. But
he wasn't.

That fact alone was completely unsettling. He was
a man who was accustomed to putting his life in
danger. He made a living from such a practice. So
why should a mere slip of a woman unsettle him so
completely?

Shying away from an answer he sensed he wasn't
quite ready to examine, he vowed to approach this
problem in a logical manner. He would plot each
angle, investigate every possibility, just as if Eleanor
Rappaport were a stunt to be choreographed.

That planning brought him to a boutique located
among the exclusive shops lining Larimer Square.

Jack sipped from the foam cup of coffee he held
and shoved his free hand deeper into his jacket. The
sky was overcast and threatened more rain. The air
hung thick with the scents of spring—damp earth,
new buds and grass. A restlessness was in the air, a
thrumming anticipation. As if there were something
waiting for him, just out of reach.

And then he saw her. Eleanor Rappaport.

She was quite lovely, he had to give her that. She
had long, thick hair the color of rich chocolate. Her
bone structure was delicate, her carriage ethereal,
her body slim and lithe. Even in the last stages of

pregnancy, she walked with the grace of a dancer, her hand resting in the crook of her mother's arm. The two of them were laughing as they came to a stop in front of Regina's shop. Victoria's Closet suited them both, with its old-world facade and vintage-style displays.

Jack slouched a little deeper into the bench where he sat. Pulling the brim of his baseball hat lower over his brow, he remained quiet and still, the coffee forgotten, as the women stopped, bussed each other on either cheek, then said their goodbyes.

It wasn't until they'd parted and Eleanor had made her way nearly a block down the street that Jack stood. From the opposite side of the street, he followed her for a hundred yards to where she stopped in front of an ornate movie theater. He saw her take a ring of keys from her pocket and open the door, then enter and lock up again.

Jack stood there a few minutes more, waiting for the lights to turn on—then realized they wouldn't be coming on. Why should they? Eleanor Rappaport didn't need them.

Drinking the last of the coffee, he tossed the cup into the garbage and retraced his steps. It was time he had some information, personal information, about Eleanor Rappaport.

"What's up, boss?"

Too late he noted that One-Eye had somehow followed him from the hotel and from there to Larimer Square.

"I thought you were going to sleep in?"

"You woke me up when you slammed the door."

"Uh-huh."

One-Eye had the grace to look sheepish, but he quickly turned the tables on Jack. "You've seen her again, haven't you? That blind woman you encountered in the restaurant."

Jack didn't answer. He began moving quickly down the street, already thinking about his next move.

"Well?" One-Eye demanded, scrambling to catch up.

"Yes," Jack confirmed shortly. "I saw her."

"So what are you going to do now?"

"I'm going to rent a car."

"What for?"

"I need to visit her landladies."

One-Eye halted in his tracks. "Her landladies! What in heaven's name for?"

ELEANOR STOOD IN THE SHADOWS just inside The Flick. The sensation had come again. That strange feeling of being watched. It had begun only a few minutes ago and hadn't eased until she'd closed herself in the theater.

Who was watching her? And why?

Growling to herself in suppressed rage, she stomped into the office, reaching for the tiny cassette recorder that was left there each day. Although she'd begun classes in Braille, Eleanor hadn't yet mastered the skill of reading the tiny bumps with the tips of her fingers, so she had been forced to find other means to circumvent the lists and books and written words she had taken for granted as a sighted person.

''Eleanor, it's Babs.'' The familiar, recorded voice spilled into the silence, filling the room with its warmth.

Barbara Worthington, the owner of The Flick, was a quick-witted, energetic woman who spent her days with her small son, Philip, and her husband, Tom, then worked during the evening hours.

Five years earlier Barbara had reopened the restored movie house under the guise of providing healthy snacks and even ''healthier'' movies—the films selected from a variety of classics and modern releases that Babs felt were ''art.'' Because of her dedication to avant-garde films, original promotional ideas, guest lecturers and community college involvement, Babs's original idea had developed a cult following. Her devoted customers guaranteed nearly full houses for its evening shows and healthy numbers of customers for the matinees, as well.

''We've got a shipment of canola oil coming just after eleven. Tell them I won't take that generic stuff they keep trying to foist on us. As far as I'm concerned, it tastes like axle grease. I want the good stuff, just as we advertise. The best they've got. After all, the Bell's Angels will be coming from the Bell Retirement Villa for the two-o'clock showing of *Magnificent Obsession*. I can't have any of them dropping in the aisle from a coronary because they ate the popcorn. Other than that, take care of the usual jobs—stocking counters, filling towel dispensers, whatever else needs to be done. Brian will be in to help you about ten-thirty. He'll take care of the cleaning and check the projectors. 'Bye.''

Replacing the recorder where she'd found it, Eleanor grimaced and reached for the wraparound apron hanging on the back door. Yet another fascinating day in the world of the cinema was about to begin. She didn't have time to think about who might be following her.

Later.

She'd think about it once she'd gone home.

ELEANOR WAS JUST CLOSING the front door to the brownstone when she heard the flap-flap of Minnie's slippers. Minnie invariably exchanged her shoes for fur-edged mules whenever she entered the house, while Maude remained in her support oxfords until she retired for bed. Thankfully, such idiosyncrasies allowed Eleanor to tell the women apart.

"Hello, Minnie."

There was a heartfelt sigh from the direction of Minnie's door. "I'm so glad you're home. I wasn't sure you would make it in time."

Eleanor frowned. "In time?"

Minnie took her hand, the elderly woman's fingers slightly cold and soft as a baby's. "These came for you."

Eleanor ran her palm over the familiar shapes of three thick books.

"The art department from the university sent them. They said that you'd agreed to evaluate them for their art history classes."

"You should have refused their proposal, Eleanor." Maude's voice chimed in from the depths of their apartment. "You're looking much too tired lately."

"I'm fine, Maude," Eleanor insisted, raising her voice to be heard. But even as she uttered the words, she resisted the urge to sigh. She *had* agreed to do this for the university, but it had been so long since the request had been made, she'd forgotten all about the arrangement. If the truth were known, she'd been sure that they would never call. Since her father was a dean at the same university, she'd suspected that the offer was made through good-natured arm twisting and not from any real need.

"A reader will be coming at seven," Minnie continued, "and it's almost that now."

Maude added, "You'll have to hurry, dear, if you want time to run a comb through your hair."

"A reader?" Eleanor echoed, wondering how all of these arrangements had been made without her input.

"Yes. Evidently there's some rush. Something about purchase orders and grants and funding. I really didn't listen too much to that part. But I did write down that a volunteer reader would be here at seven." She patted Eleanor's hand. "I met your reader earlier today. We had a cup of tea together and chatted for a few minutes."

Eleanor scowled in irritation. She'd been assigned several volunteer readers from the university over the past few months. After dealing with the young students, she'd come to the conclusion that she preferred to choose her own assistants. Some of the kids sent her way could barely read themselves, others had annoying voices or distracting habits. A reader was much like a car. It needed to be test-driven before becoming a permanent part of one's life.

But Minnie wasn't to blame for the situation, so there was no sense in Eleanor venting her irritation.

"Thank you for your help, Minnie," she managed to say. "If you'll just stack the books on my arm."

The collection of art history texts weighed nearly ten pounds, but Eleanor was able to make the climb to the third-floor landing without too much difficulty.

Because the four-story brownstone had been altered from its original one-family dwelling into a two-apartment complex, Minnie and Maude had the first two floors for their own use, and Eleanor had the top two.

Twisting the knob, Eleanor entered the living room and dumped the books and her purse on the couch by the door. Although she was not a vain woman, she wished she had more time before the reader was expected. One of the volunteers she'd used a few months ago had commented on the "dustiness" of Eleanor's furnishings. Until that encounter, Eleanor hadn't paid much attention to her living quarters. She kept her belongings neat out of necessity, but dusting wasn't her strong suit.

Her fingers ran lightly over the chair rail along the wall as she hurried into her bedroom, brushed her hair, twisted it into a French knot and secured it with an ornate clip her mother had given her years ago. Then she threw off the sweater and maternity jeans she'd worn to work, exchanging them for a lighter cotton dress. Minnie and Maude liked their apartment to be warm—almost tropical. Even with her own thermostat off, Eleanor's rooms tended to get quite hot.

She was making her way to the bathroom to attempt a bit of blush and eye shadow when the doorbell rang.

"Blast it all," she muttered under her breath. Why hadn't the university at least called to see if this evening would be convenient for such an activity? The last thing Eleanor wanted that night was hours of listening to some gum-popping, barely out-of-high-school teenager stumbling her way through an art history tome.

The doorbell rang again, then was followed by a sharp rap on the panels.

"Coming," she called out impatiently. If first impressions were worth anything, Eleanor was ready to send the woman packing. After all, this was Eleanor's home. She shouldn't be summoned to the door as if she were some sort of inconvenience to this girl's valuable time.

Piqued, Eleanor threw the door open. "Listen, I realize that you're new at this, but if the two of us are going to work together, there are a few ground rules you'll need to follow."

"Fine."

The voice wasn't that of a woman. It was very dark, very low.

And very male.

Chapter Four

Eleanor's irritation fizzled out, and she felt her cheeks grow hot when she realized that her visitor was a man. One with a voice that was rich as molasses.

Her head tilted and she stood for several seconds, absorbing what she could from senses that had grown keener since her accident but still could not reassure her as much as a quick visual study had once done.

"*You* were sent by the university?" she asked.

"I'm the reader."

No. This would never do.

Eleanor folded her arms over her stomach, holding a protective hand to the spot where even the baby kicked in alarm—telling body language, she knew, but she couldn't help it. She'd been expecting a woman. The university had *always* sent women in the past—Eleanor herself had made such a request. She didn't want to open herself up to the complications inherent in inviting a man into her life. In her experience, men were...well, different. They had odd expectation levels. They tended to be brusque, unemotional, impatient and didactic. She didn't want that kind of baggage in a reader.

"There must be some mistake, Mr...."

"You can call me Jack."

She didn't want to call him anything. She didn't want him in her house, reading in that low, lazy, drawling sort of voice—a voice that sounded strangely familiar....

No. She wanted someone of her own sex, someone who would be decidedly safer.

Safer?

"Jack, then," she said grudgingly. She really would have preferred knowing his last name. There was something more professional about firing a person by using last names. "There must have been some mistake. I can assure you I—"

"No mistake."

He shifted, and Eleanor started when the action brought with it a whiff of a clean, woodsy cologne. The delicate hairs on her arms stood on end. She felt the warmth of his body and knew that he must be standing close. Very close.

"Mr...."

"Call me Jack," he said again.

Sighing, she stepped out of the way, knowing that she would have to consult with the university about changing readers. Until then she needed to make the best of the situation.

"Come on in, Jack."

She felt him brush past her, and her skin tingled from the brief contact.

"The books are on the couch. Have a seat."

The old settee creaked comfortably as he settled onto the cushions.

Eleanor made her way to the overstuffed chair opposite. She could thank her mother for decorating the apartment. While Eleanor had been in rehabilitation, Regina had seen to it that Eleanor's things were moved out of Roger's condo. Originally, Regina had insisted that Eleanor move in with her, since Regina and Eleanor's father were divorced. But Eleanor had been adamant about maintaining at least some part of her independence, so Regina had contacted her godmothers, obtained this apartment—the same one she'd rented during her college years—and had arranged Eleanor's belongings with a minimum of clutter.

"You were going to tell me your ground rules."

The velvety tones brought Eleanor back to the present with a jolt.

"If we continue to work together—"

"If?"

Eleanor sighed. Already, she sensed Jack was an "interrupter." She hated people who wouldn't let her finish her sentences.

"*If* we continue to work together, I will expect you to be prompt and adaptable to changes in my schedule. I will also expect you to have a rudimentary pronunciation of the names and subjects involved."

What she didn't tell him was that she wasn't really considering him for the position.

"Fine."

"*If* I am satisfied with the relationship, there is a possibility that I may ask you to help with some other reading work. Should that prove to be the case, I will pay you an hourly wage in accordance with the current rate."

"That's not necessary. I volunteered for the position."

Eleanor tamped down the frustration she felt at being the recipient of such charity. She couldn't help thinking that there were other people far more deserving or needy of volunteer services. She had her family or her landladies to help her. Even Brian and Babs were willing to read when things were slow.

But not three sets of text books.

She sighed. No. She doubted there was anyone on the face of the earth who would willingly read three art history books.

"Mr.—"

"Jack. Jack MacAllister. But I wish you'd call me Jack."

Why was she having such a hard time using his first name? Why did it seem overly familiar?

"I don't suppose that you have an artistic background?" she asked wearily.

"Yes, ma'am, I do."

The unexpected answer caused her head to tilt.

"Really? In what area?"

"Film."

It wasn't exactly what she needed for the current project, but Eleanor supposed that even a student of cinema would be required to take courses in basic composition.

"What do you do, Jack?" she asked.

"When?"

Her lips twitched at the purposely obtuse answer. She caught the hint of teasing in his tone.

"When you're not reading for strange blind women."

"I'm on vacation."

"From what."

"Working."

"Oh, really?" she said drolly. "And what might that be?"

"I jump off things."

The statement was so startling that Eleanor could find no immediate response.

"Beg pardon?"

"I jump off things. I'm a stuntman."

"Locally?"

"I...freelance a lot."

She frowned. "You're serious? Can a person make a living doing something like that?"

"You'd be surprised."

Deciding he was teasing her again, she dropped the line of questioning.

"Why have you volunteered to be my reader, Jack?"

"I needed something to do."

"So you got out of bed one morning and said to yourself, 'Hey, let's find a blind lady with a lot of big books.'"

"Something like that."

"There are other ways to relieve boredom."

"That's probably true, but I chose this as my diversion of choice."

"Other than your studies, you mean?"

He didn't answer and she took his silence as an affirmative remark, knowing that if he had nodded, she would have missed the gesture. She wished that she could see the tilt of his body. She missed being able to interpret subtle, body-language cues she had grown so accustomed to using to her advantage when meeting someone new.

"Why should I keep you as my reader, Jack?"

Eleanor was not normally so blunt, but there was something about this man, about the way he sounded so self-assured, so almost…arrogant, that made her think the shocking lack of manners would help her to measure him more fully.

She felt, rather than heard, the way he leaned forward. She could almost picture what he must look like, tall, lean, propping his elbows on his knees. He was probably broodingly dark or elegantly blond. Something to match that voice. That incredible voice.

"You should keep me, because you need my help."

"I would think that particular point was obvious, Jack. But why do I need *you?*"

The moment the question had been uttered, she found herself wishing she hadn't been so bold. A curious silence had begun to flood the room in ever-widening ripples. One that was somehow invigorating and frightening at the same time. She had never encountered such a sensation before, an aura of energy that began to infuse her body so completely that she found her mouth growing dry and her breathing shallow.

"You need what I can give you."

She waited, praying he would elaborate and set her fears at ease before her mind began to insinuate all sorts of subtle shadings to that remark.

"You need my insight. My passion."

"Passion?" she could barely force the words from her throat.

"My passion for the subject."

"Oh, yes." She cleared her throat, to relieve it of the husky quality it had adopted. "But I thought you said your specialty was film."

"It's all the same, isn't it? Light and shadow, composition and form. The raw expression of emotion."

Eleanor had never heard a definition that was so simple, yet so powerful. But then, she had never met anyone like Jack. Since walking into her narrow apartment, he'd filled the room with his vitality, as well as a sense of purpose that she found difficult to assimilate.

When he touched her hand, she started.

"What are you doing?" She hadn't meant for her voice to emerge with such temerity and...

And what? Fascination?

"I frighten you."

The statement was so near the truth she immediately denied it. "No, of course not."

"Then I worry you, at the very least."

He hadn't released her. Indeed, he was pulling her closer, causing her to sit on the edge of her seat.

"Maybe it would help if you had a better picture of what I look like."

She realized then that he was giving her the opportunity to Braille his face.

Lifting both hands, she allowed him to position them on either side of his head. Softly, expertly, she began to search the features with the same curiosity she had once used to examine marble statues at some of the finest museums in the world.

But this man was different. He didn't have the rounded features of the Greeks, or the noble simplicity of the Romans. His hair was soft and fine, longer on top, but cut very short at the sides. His forehead was wide and square, his brows sharply defined, his nose slender, his cheeks high and sharp, his chin angular, and his lips...

She shuddered, a warmth beginning to radiate from deep in her belly as Jack's mouth parted and he exhaled, causing his breath to whisper over her sensitive fingertips.

"Is that better?" he said against her.

Eleanor's heart had begun to pound in a slow, measured thud.

No, it was worse. So much worse.

"Your hair," she whispered. "What color is your hair?"

Despite the fact that her voice sounded far too needy in her own ears, she had to know the entire picture. She had to *see* him.

"Dark brown."

Like molasses. Like his voice.

"Your eyes?"

"Dark brown."

She fought the burgeoning wariness filtering through her veins, filling her with a languid heat. It wasn't right to be responding this way to a volunteer. It wasn't in the least bit businesslike.

But dear Heaven above, she was beginning to form an image of him in her head that wouldn't go away. The clarity of her imagination was strange and disturbing, as if somewhere, somehow, she'd seen him. And that voice...

"Do I know you?" The question slipped from her lips before she had a chance to think about what she was asking. If she could have retrieved the preposterous question, she would have done so. After all, she would have remembered the identity of someone with such an unusual voice.

Jack didn't immediately respond to the question, and she would have brushed it away if not for the way the features beneath her fingers had grown tense and still and completely expressionless.

Again the second thoughts she'd experienced since his arrival resurfaced. She didn't need the inherent complications involved in working with a man who so clearly...

So clearly what? Attracted her?

"No. You don't know me. We met once. Yesterday, as a matter of fact."

"The man who retrieved my scarf," she said softly, finally pinpointing the strange familiarity of his voice.

"Yes."

Jack's explanation should have relieved her—after all, he'd been quite kind to have helped her last evening. But it didn't. Instead, she was remembering the warmth that had flooded her body when he'd touched her shoulder the night before.

Pulling sharply away, she folded her hands in her lap and said primly, "I don't think this is going to work, Jack."

"Why?"

"I don't believe I have to give any reasons. It's merely a gut feeling I have."

"Would that 'gut feeling' be feminine intuition? Or fear?"

Fear? She wasn't sure that she would use such a strong word.

"I'm not afraid of you," she said sharply.

"I didn't think you were. I think you're afraid of the situation."

His comment had the ability to blast away her vulnerability with a burst of pique. Jumping to her feet, she made her way to the window. The air had grown unbearably close and stuffy and charged with an awareness she didn't want to acknowledge.

"What situation is that, Jack?"

Finding the sash just where she'd known it would be, she tried to lift it, but the rain had caused the wood to swell, making the runners stick.

"The fact that I'm a man, when you are accustomed to dealing with females."

Eleanor started. He'd followed her so silently, she hadn't realized he was directly behind her.

Brushing her aside, he lifted the window, allowing a slight draft to ease into the room. The cooler air wasn't nearly as comforting as she had thought it would be.

Eleanor folded her arms under her breasts. "Are you always this outspoken, Jack?"

"Yes."

Again his candidness surprised her. This time, when his thumb and forefinger caught her chin, she didn't jump. She'd been expecting him to touch her. She'd *known* he would touch her.

"Give me a chance, Eleanor Rappaport. One week."

"Three nights."

"One week."

"I don't work on the weekends, so you have five days."

This time she felt him nod, heard the soft rustle of his clothing. His thumb released her chin, so slowly that she could feel it brush against the lower curve of her lip.

"It's a deal."

He took her hand, his grip firm and strong and faintly callused. She wondered if he knew how much that hand told her about him. That he was a man who worked hard and was accustomed to keeping his promises.

When he finally released her, she heard him turn away and make his way to the couch. But she did not hear the rustling of the cushions.

"I'll see you tomorrow about seven again."

Eleanor's mouth dropped. Shouldn't she be the one to determine when their session was finished?

"I beg your pardon?"

"Is seven all right?"

"Yes, but..."

He was there beside her again, touching her chin and forcing it to close. "We've done all we can for tonight."

"I don't know how you jumped to such a conclusion."

"While we've been talking, the light has changed. It's almost pitch-black in here."

"So I'll turn on a lamp." Eleanor knew every inch of her apartment, every space, every nook, every cranny. Marching to the switch, she flicked it on.

"Nothing happened."

Not sure if she should believe him or not, she tugged on the chain on the table lamp.

"Still nothing."

Sighing in irritation, she plunked her hands on her hips, only to hear his soft chuckle.

"Don't knock yourself out. The bulbs are burned out."

"So you're a psychic now, too?"

"Not at all. One of your landladies warned me— Minnie is it?"

She nodded, and he continued.

"About a week ago—after your mother had visited—Minnie noticed that all the lights were left on in your apartment. She meant to warn you, but the fact slipped her mind until she saw me this evening.

Since she hadn't noticed any lights for some time, she was afraid the bulbs had burned out.''

Eleanor felt a creeping tide of heat climb her cheeks.

The door to the hall squeaked open, signaling Jack's departure. When she didn't hear his footfalls in the hall, she stiffened, sensing that he was approaching her again.

His fingers stroked her hair, she grew still.

"Don't worry about it, Eleanor. You couldn't have known."

Even so, she damned herself for that telling error. One that had informed him quite eloquently that she was...

Blind? He already knew that. It was the reason why he'd come here in the first place.

"So serious and so proud."

She barely caught the words, they were uttered so softly.

With a twist of her head, she severed the contact between them.

He chuckled. "I get the message. Hands off."

"Ours is to be a professional relationship."

"Is it."

The words weren't really a question, but she couldn't imagine any man making sexual overtures to a blind woman with a stomach the size of a beach ball.

"Tomorrow, then." She felt him move into the hall. "And do one thing more for me. Wear your hair down. I'd like to see it down."

Before she could respond, the door had clicked shut.

Leaving her outraged.

And just a little bit pleased.

Chapter Five

Wear your hair down. I'd like to see it down.

Of all the nerve. Of all the complete and utter nerve! As if Eleanor cared one bit what Jack What-ever-His-Last-Name-Was wanted her to do with her hair. How dare he order her about in any way at all? After all, she was the person in charge, and he was the volunteer. Right?

Right.

"There you are, Miss Rappaport."

The bus whined to a stop.

"Thanks, Burt."

Eleanor waited for the thump of the back doors to open, then descended to the curb, carrying a huge sack of lightbulbs in one hand and her cane in the other.

As soon as her toe touched the pavement, she rang her bicycle bell for Burt's benefit, then began to march toward the brownstone, fuming the entire way.

If the truth were known, she'd chided herself every waking minute for agreeing to work with Jack that evening—or any other evening, for that matter. The man was far too high-handed and arrogant for her needs. She should have called the university and demanded a replacement.

Even though she'd been tempted to do that at least a half dozen times, she never had. Mainly, she'd known that he'd probably been chosen to work with her because he had a passing knowledge of artistic terms—and in that area, beggars couldn't afford to be choosers.

Nevertheless, this evening she intended to put him in his place. She had enough lightbulbs—of every size, watt, and hue—to light the town hall inside and out. Before Jack arrived, she intended to have all of the lamps and fixtures in the apartment fitted with fresh bulbs—whether or not they needed one. Then she would change into a conservative suit, draw her hair to her nape in an elegant and refined chignon, and *dare* him to make a comment about it.

"Here, let me take that from you."

Eleanor had just touched the stoop's lower step with the tip of her cane when the voice melted out of the blackness around her. As her eyes closed in disbelief, there was no denying the owner of those husky tones. In an instant she was so attuned to Jack's presence she could hear the infinitesimal squeak of his boots and the rustle of his clothing as he stood. His soles scraped the concrete as he came toward her. With each step a strange energy began to radiate through her muscles.

"What are you doing here?"

"My goodness, what gracious manners," he teased.

Her lips thinned, even though she deserved the chastisement.

"It isn't even six o'clock yet," she noted.

"I didn't have anything else to do, so I decided to drop by and help you with the lightbulbs." There was a tug at the paper sack, and she relinquished it—but only because she didn't want to be seen having a tug-of-war by anyone who passed by.

"Did it occur to you that I might not be home?" she asked defiantly.

"Sure. But you're home now," he said.

Eleanor considered losing her temper at his abrupt reply—or at the very least scolding him for his lack of manners. But somehow, she sensed it wouldn't do any good.

"Come on up," she suggested grudgingly.

She heard the creak of the door, and Jack said, "After you."

Folding her cane, she made her way to the stairwell and from there to her third-floor apartment.

Since she meant to put him in his proper place right from the start, she inquired, "Did you have a chance to go over the texts?"

"I skimmed the first few chapters. I hope you didn't expect me to read them all the first night."

"Hardly. We'll have to take some readability tests tonight. That will take some time."

"Fine. I've got all the time in the world."

Obviously, since he was here on her doorstep instead of pursuing his own ends for another hour.

Letting him inside, she made a wide gesture. "If you were serious about changing the bulbs, knock yourself out."

"All right."

The sack rustled, there was a thump, and the cushions of the couch squeaked—presumably as he dropped the books.

"In the meantime, I need to take a shower and get out of these clothes." She gestured to the maternity jeans and oversize sweater she wore.

"Remember what I said about your hair."

Eleanor had been halfway across the room when she heard his comment, and she whirled in his direction. "Somehow I doubt that my hair should even be an issue this evening, Mr...."

"Jack."

She whipped her dark glasses from her face and tossed them onto the bar that separated the kitchen from the living room.

"Look. Maybe I didn't make myself clear enough last night, but if this is going to work, our relationship has to stay on a purely professional footing."

"You can't be professional with your hair down?"

She huffed in irritation, striding to where the warmth of the late-evening sunshine streamed through the windows. "The whole subject is preposterous. It shouldn't matter to you what I do."

This time she heard him approach, not because he made any noise himself, but because the creak of the floorboards betrayed him.

Before she knew what he meant to do, he had

turned her to face him and cupped her face in his hands.

"It matters to me, because I know why you don't like to wear it down."

"So you're crossing into the realms of mind reading again, eh?"

"Not at all. It doesn't take a psychic to see the way you try to hide yourself." Again, she sensed a teasing note to his inflection.

"Hide myself?" she echoed indignantly.

"On each of the occasions I've seen you, your hair has been scraped back in some awful librarian's knot and your body's been camouflaged by shapeless sweaters."

"Now you're a fashion critic, as well? It might have escaped your notice, but I'm pregnant, and shapeless sweaters are about as fashion conscious as a woman in my condition is likely to get."

"I just think that it's a crime to disguise anyone as lovely as you. Your pregnancy merely heightens your beauty."

The words shuddered in the room around her, causing her breath to lock in her throat.

Jack's grip gentled, and he tipped her head to the warmth of the dying light.

"Don't hide from it. Don't deny it."

She jerked away, taking a step, then stopping. Not because he had physically restrained her, but because she didn't have the strength to go any further. The air in the apartment had become sticky with some nameless emotion. A yearning. An awareness. A need.

"You don't believe me, do you?" he asked from behind.

Since she had no other choice, she was brutally honest with him. "I haven't seen myself in a mirror in quite some time. I don't know what I look like."

"You weren't born blind."

It was a statement, not a question, but she answered it nonetheless. "No. I was involved in a car accident several months ago. It was no one's fault. Just an icy road and the bad luck of being in the wrong place at the wrong time. I've lived here ever since. But as you've probably already noticed by Minnie's dated wardrobe and Maude's garish wigs, I can't really rely on their opinions of my appearance."

She felt him touch her arm with a single finger, stroking up and down the light weave of her sweater in a way that should have been comforting, but had the ability to arouse far baser emotions instead. Such as want. Hunger.

"Where did you live before?"

Not about to bare her soul to a total stranger, she avoided all mention of Roger and said, "I was in a condo near Estes Park, but considering the circumstances and my condition my parents thought it would be best to live closer to my doctors and the hospital. Naturally, my mother wanted me to live with her, but I insisted on my own place."

"And you're...alone here?"

She knew what he was asking...if an irate husband was about to burst onto the scene.

She hesitated, then finally admitted, "My fiancé

wasn't too pleased when he discovered our birth control measures had not been one-hundred percent fool-proof. Evidently, he found my blindness an added incentive for breaking off the long-standing engagement.''

"I'm sorry."

She shrugged. "Don't be. I see now that it was all for the best. Roger and I grew apart years ago, but we were so much in the habit of being a couple that we failed to see that the relationship was quickly heading downhill." She grimaced. "Roger never wanted children." She patted her stomach. "So it's best for both of us that he's out of the picture."

Now why had she told him that? The information was really far too personal to be passing along to a casual stranger. He didn't need to know about the soul-searching she'd done after Roger's desertion. Nor did he need to know how her accident had changed her baby's life as much as her own. To her infinite shame after discovering she was pregnant, Eleanor had avoided thinking about her condition as anything other than a chink in her relationship with Roger. It hadn't been until she'd recovered from the shock and disorientation of the accident that she had grown keenly aware of the life she carried. In that instant, she knew that she wanted her baby, that she already loved it beyond measure.

"Your apartment is nice." The finger moved from her elbow to her shoulder, then to her neck.

It took all the will she possessed not to lean into

the pressure, to give in to the inherent possibilities it represented.

"Do you regret living here with Minnie and Maude?"

"No. Not really."

"Then you've made a place for yourself here."

Again, it wasn't a question. But this time the words made her think hard. Had she made a place for herself? She supposed. She had an apartment to live in, a job, people who cared for her. But other than that, she existed. She merely existed.

"I need to change."

She stepped away from his warmth so abruptly that it was like severing herself from a tangible bond.

But once at the doorway to the hall, she paused. "You'll wait here for me?"

She didn't know why she felt compelled to ask. She knew he would probably misinterpret and think she'd feared he would follow her to her bedroom. But the opposite was true. At that moment she was more afraid that he would leave, that he would decide she was too damned ornery to spend time with.

"I'll be here."

JACK WATCHED HER GO, his eyes narrowed and assessing. Then, when Eleanor was out of sight, he listened to her footfalls in the hall and the bump of her door closing.

She was incredible.

Beautiful.

Angry.

Vulnerable.

And so very complex.

Sighing, he grabbed the paper sack and withdrew several of the containers of bulbs, wondering what had possessed him to get so involved with a stranger.

Only yesterday he'd driven to the brownstone after renting a car. As he'd studied the area, he'd seen one of Eleanor's landladies struggling to bring her garbage cans out to the curb. When he'd gone to her assistance, the woman had begun to tell him all about her home and her beautiful tenant. It was then that Jack had learned about the reader who was expected to arrive some time that evening.

Pretending to be that reader, he had been invited inside for tea and had been given more information on Eleanor Rappaport than he would have thought possible. From Minnie Vanderbilt, he'd learned that Eleanor had once been a world-famous artist and that she'd been preparing for a showing at the National Gallery when the accident had occurred. Minnie had told him all about Eleanor's recuperation and rehabilitation, about the man who had fathered Eleanor's child and deserted her, her current job and her status as a technical advisor to the university's art department.

But gazing around him now at the brownstone apartment, he knew deep in his soul that the people in Eleanor's life had been so concerned about her physical adaptation to her sightlessness that they had overlooked a far more basic adjustment.

The rooms about him were beautiful, arranged

with a decorator's instinct. Beyond that they were
sterile. There was no evidence of life here, no trin-
kets of passion or amusement—no real signs of the
imminent birth of her baby. There was no art—and
for a woman who had been an artist, that fact was
the most telling of all. Granted, she could not have
enjoyed paintings or vibrant color schemes, but there
were no tactile embellishments, either. No knick-
knacks, no sculptures, no flowers, no personal par-
aphernalia.

That element worried him far more than anything
else he had seen yet. This was not a home, it was a
prison. A comfortable one, he would admit, but a
prison nonetheless. He would wager that Eleanor left
this spot each morning, made her way to work, then
returned with as little deviation as possible.

A perfect survival technique.

But a hell of a way to live.

After finishing with the fixtures in the living
room, Jack exchanged all the bulbs in the kitchen,
taking a minute to glance in the cupboards and the
refrigerator. Just as he'd thought, only the barest es-
sentials had been purchased.

"Dammit all to hell," he whispered to himself.

"What?"

He started when Eleanor stepped through the
doorway. He'd been so busy in his search for clues,
he hadn't heard her approach.

Automatically, he scanned her from top to toe.
Her hair was down, but pulled back in a loose
plait—something he would work on in the future.
Her jeans and sweater had been exchanged for a pair

of loose linen trousers and what looked like an over-size vintage shirt. Better. So much better.

"You look great," he said softly, knowing that if he said the wrong thing, he would startle her. She was barely beginning to accept him. And he would have to take things slowly before...

Before what? He wasn't really sure what objective he sought with Eleanor Rappaport.

"You're full of flattery tonight, Jack," she said dismissingly, striding into the living room. On her way, she paused at the counter to locate her sunglasses and put them back on the bridge of her nose.

He frowned, following her much more slowly. "Why did you do that?"

She stopped in front of a table lamp. The glow settled around her like a golden aura, causing him to stare. How was it that a man like him, who was used to associating with teamsters and stage hands, had stumbled into her world?

"Do what?" she countered, even though Jack was sure she knew what he'd been referring to.

"Why did you put your glasses back on?"

She didn't answer, but he saw the way her shoulders drew back in a faint, militant line.

"Can you see the light?" he demanded. "Any of it?"

It was obvious that she didn't want to answer, but she finally offered, "Sometimes I can determine a very bright light, yes."

"Can you see it tonight?"

It was obvious that she wanted to answer in the

affirmative, just as it was obvious that to do so would be a lie.

"No."

"Then why the glasses?" He was slowly approaching her, knowing that she must feel him growing near. She *had* to feel it. He only had to enter the same room as she to perceive her presence in the way his body became aware, his senses more in tune. Surely, she must be experiencing something similar.

"Why the glasses, Eleanor?"

She sighed. "My eyes are…unpleasant to look at."

He was stunned that she would think such a thing. "Who told you that?"

He was so close to her now, he could feel her nervousness.

"I didn't need to be told."

"So you assumed that because no one had ever said anything, that your eyes were scarred?"

"Yes." The word resonated with her irritation.

When she would have turned away from him, he caught her elbow, forcing her to be still.

"Then, you're wrong. So very wrong." He gently slid the glasses from her face and tossed them onto the couch. Cupping her cheeks, he lifted her face to the light, staring deep into the same eyes he'd studied so long ago on a frantic mountain highway.

Suddenly she was gripping his wrists. "Don't lie to me, Jack." The warning was raw and filled with emotion. "I need to know the truth. I asked my mother once, but I could never trust her answer.

She's always trying to shield me from unpleasantness."

"What did she say?"

"That they were 'fine.'"

"Then she was wrong." He felt the way she stiffened and added softly, "Your eyes aren't fine. They're beautiful. Never in my life have I seen such a warm shade of blue—almost pansy colored. Rich. Clear."

She trembled in his arms like a bird that had been liberated from the cold.

"But your eyes are only part of the whole," he continued, wondering where he'd found the words to explain what he'd been thinking from the moment he'd seen her in the rain. "Your hair is soft and baby fine—thick and rich and the color of a faun's. Your skin is incredible, your lips full. But no matter where a man looks, he will always be drawn back to those eyes. To the fire that's still buried inside them."

The room grew so silent they could both hear the faint ticking of a clock and the creak of the house as it settled for the night.

Looking down at her, Jack admitted to himself that he wanted to kiss her—that he *needed* to kiss her. But he also knew that such an action would destroy the moment. It was too soon for such physicality. Much too soon. He would have to wait until the moment was right. Until then, he had this instant, this short embrace.

It was Eleanor who stepped free first. She turned

away, obviously embarrassed. "You probably think I'm pitiful."

Pity.

She was incredibly leery of that emotion. He knew that from the set of her shoulders and the jut of her chin.

"Not at all." He kept his tone light and teasing. "I think you're cautious, suspicious—and maybe even bossy—but I would never think you were pitiful."

Her lips quirked in a reluctant smile.

"Thank you, Dr. Jack."

"Not at all."

He took her hand, drawing her to the chair she had used the night before. "What do you say we get to work?"

She took her place with such alacrity, he knew he'd been right to put things back on a businesslike footing.

Taking his own seat on the couch, he opened the first text book and began to read the information she would require about the publishing and copyright dates.

But through it all, he couldn't help thinking…

Tomorrow. Tomorrow, we'll take things one step further.

Chapter Six

"I've found us some digs, Jack," One-Eye said as Jack entered the hotel room they shared.

"What do you mean?" he asked, suddenly weary. Shrugging out of his jacket, he tossed it onto the bed, then sat on the side to remove his shoes.

"Well, I got to thinking about what you said yesterday—about the way you'd changed your mind and wanted to stay in Denver for a while longer."

"Yeah," Jack prompted, unbuttoning his shirt.

"I got to thinking about Victor Russo."

Jack paused. "Victor?"

Victor Russo had been a fellow stuntman on a movie Jack and One-Eye had made the previous year.

"He asked us to come visit him sometime. Remember?"

Jack frowned. "I think the offer included skiing. There's no snow, One-Eye."

"He didn't seem to mind when I called him."

Again, Jack stared at his companion. "You called him?"

"Sure. Neither one of us is made of money, and I'm getting tired of eating from vending machines two times a day."

"What did Victor say?"

"He invited us to dinner—his treat!" One-Eye said with excitement. "And he insisted we stay with him afterwards."

"You're sure he didn't mind?"

"He's glad we took him up on his offer."

"I'll be damned," Jack murmured. By staying at Victor's house, he would be able to extend his visit by a week. Maybe two.

Whoa!

"That's not the best part," One-Eye continued. "Victor's giving a party day after tomorrow—some big studio is making a movie here in town, and he's schmoozing the director. He's invited us to come, as well." He chortled. "He even volunteered to get you a date, if you'd like."

Jack shoved his hands in his jeans pockets. His mind was immediately flooded with the possibilities of a crowded room and Eleanor on his arm.

"Well? What do you say?"

"I think I can find my own date, One-Eye."

One-Eye cackled in glee. "I take it you'll be bringing the Rappaport woman?"

"Maybe."

"I thought so," One-Eye said knowingly. Scooping his clothes from a pile on the bed, he made his way to the bathroom. "I'll shower first."

Jack didn't move. Already his mind was racing with plans. Tomorrow he would rent another car for his stay. Then he intended to scout the blocks surrounding Eleanor's home. Hopefully, he could find some points of interest near enough to draw her out of her apartment. If not...

Well, he would have to come up with something. He didn't know why, but he felt the need to get her out of that house. An overwhelming need. What he wanted was a place that had dancing. Music. Hot dogs and lemonade.

Going to the closet to gather his clothes, Jack decided the whole idea might not be half-bad.

ELEANOR TOOK MUCH LONGER than usual to get home the next evening. A craft fair was taking place at Larimer Square, and in honor of the occasion most of the shops and boutiques were having sales. The ensuing pedestrian traffic made Eleanor's navigation to the bus stop all but impossible. Once on the bus, the aisle had been so crowded with other commuters intent on getting home, that she'd been forced to cling to the overhead rail. As the five-minute ride stretched to twenty, she prayed she wouldn't suffocate before she could pry herself loose from a tall bare-armed man smelling of sweat and a chattering teenager reeking of cheap perfume.

By the time she stepped onto the curb at her stop and rang her bicycle bell, her nerves were raw and her temper was ready to boil. Too late she realized she hadn't eaten her usual snack at midday. The pace at the theater had been frantic. Now she was hungry, slightly nauseous, cross, tired—

And in no mood to deal with Mr. Jack Mac-Allister.

"Hello, Eleanor."

She supposed that the voice coming to her from the top of the stoop should have been inevitable. Nonetheless, she couldn't help the heavy sigh.

"Hello, Jack."

Suddenly weary, she sank onto one of the steps and turned her face up to the cool breeze. She wasn't completely sure, but in its moistness she thought she caught the first real hint of spring.

"You're early again," she stated needlessly.

She heard the rustling of his clothing, then felt him take the narrow space beside her.

"I told you. I'm on vacation. I don't have anything else to do."

"Well, I do," she insisted.

"Such as?"

Such as what? She couldn't claim an appointment or a previous engagement. If she told him the truth, that she wanted to sit back, breathe deeply and munch on a peanut butter sandwich, she was sure that he would insist on joining her, so she shrugged, refusing to answer.

"Actually I came early for a reason," he said after it became apparent that she didn't intend to respond.

"What kind of reason?"

"I thought you might like to join me for something to eat."

Food. Hearty, warm, satisfying food.

"I've had my fill of the stuff I've been getting out of a machine lately, and I thought I'd—"

"You've been eating out of a machine?" she interrupted.

"Sure."

"How can anyone possibly eat from a machine?"

"You know, chips, sodas, sandwiches."

Eleanor gripped his leg, then immediately regretted the spontaneous action and let go. It was rock hard.

"I take it your diet is usually more strict."

"Why would you say that?" There was a hint of humor in his tone, as if he knew exactly what had possessed her to be so bold. She prayed he hadn't caught the quick inhalation she'd made when the warmth of his body had shot into her chilled fingers.

"You seem athletic," she answered noncommittally, not about to convict herself with a more personal response.

"My work keeps me in shape."

"Your work?" she echoed. She was growing increasingly aware of the way his shoulder brushed hers and how their thighs very nearly touched.

"I jump off things, remember?"

She hadn't remembered, but she supposed that her forgetfulness had been due in part to the fact that she hadn't thought he was completely serious.

"Are you part of the movie being filmed outside town?"

"No, but I know some of the crews involved."

She shook her head in disbelief. "Are there enough movies made here for you to…freelance?"

she asked, remembering that was the word he had
used to describe his means of employment.

"I travel a good deal."

"Oh." For some reason the thought made her
hollow inside. "How do you keep up with your
studies?"

There was a slight pause in the rhythm of their
conversation, then Jack offered, "I manage." He
shifted, causing her to become aware of his shape,
his form, his scent—a fragrance that she recognized
as the same cologne her father used to use.

"Do you want to go with me to get something to
eat?"

They'd strayed so far from the original thrust of
their conversation, that Eleanor had to drag her mind
back to the matter at hand. How was it possible for
this man to scatter her wits every time she was in
his company?

"I don't think I'd better," she said regretfully,
surprising herself by how truly disappointed she
was.

"Why not?"

"I've got a splitting headache."

"We'll get you some aspirin."

"I had a horrible day."

"So a night out will do you good."

"We have all those books to read."

"A meal isn't going to take that much time."

"I'd be horrible company."

"You couldn't be horrible if you tried." His finger grazed her cheek, causing a tingling sensation to

spread from that point of contact through her entire body, warming her, relaxing her.

"Come on, Eleanor," he coaxed, his voice so low, so deep and compelling and she gripped her cane to keep from dropping it.

"I've got a nice place in mind. A little Italian joint a few blocks away. We'll have some hot soup, bread, pasta."

Eleanor's stomach growled in delight, and she prayed he hadn't heard it.

"Please?" he whispered. "I don't want to be alone."

The words shimmied through her with such power there was no way she could resist.

"Lead the way."

JACK STOOD, all the while wondering if he should take Eleanor's arm. Her hand?

In the end his hesitation didn't matter. She stood quickly—perhaps even to prevent such help—and unfolded her cane with an efficiency that bordered on being manic.

"Where to?" she asked curtly.

"My car's over here."

"Car?"

"It's too cold to walk."

He knew she was relieved the moment he offered the explanation. Despite her guardedness, she'd been easy to read. He watched as she rose stiffly from the stoop. Not for the first time he wondered about the toll pregnancy must be taking on her already-strained emotional and physical health.

"You look exhausted," Jack said as she joined him on the sidewalk.

"I am." She hesitated, then said, "Since I don't know where your car is located, this whole experience would be easier if you'd let me take your elbow."

"Sure."

Her reluctance was obvious as she slid her fingers around his biceps and allowed him to lead her farther down the street.

"Are you a native of Denver, Jack?"

"No. I've only been here a short time." Briefly he considered informing her just how "short" his stay had been, but he shrugged the impulse away. Now wasn't the time to make heartfelt confessions. One wrong move, one wrong word, and this woman would retreat so fast his head would spin. "Originally I'm from Virginia."

"Oh, really?"

She didn't offer anything more, and since they had approached his rental car, Jack didn't press her. There would be time enough for confidences before the evening was through.

"Here we are." He bent to unlock the low-slung Corvette, then held open the door.

She quickly folded her cane, then moved into the lee of the door, her fingers nimbly searching the car's exterior.

"You have expensive tastes, Jack."

"How can you tell?"

"Only a sports car would be this low."

She sank into the seat and after he'd made sure

her seat belt was fastened, he went around to his own side of the car.

"I wish I could claim it as my own," he said as he gunned the engine.

"Someone actually let you borrow this thing?"

"He doesn't know me very well," he countered. After moving into Victor's apartment, his friend had insisted that Jack use his spare car instead of renting one. When he'd agreed, he hadn't known he'd be driving a candy-apple-red 'Vette. Originally Jack had been concerned that the car might be awkward for a pregnant woman, but Eleanor didn't seem to have any problems getting in—and he'd have an excuse to help her get out.

The drive to the restaurant was short, and Jack couldn't help but congratulate himself on the fact, when he heard the faint growling of Eleanor's stomach. After her earlier bravado, that hint of vulnerability intrigued him.

"Do you still need the aspirin?" he asked after he'd parked and opened Eleanor's door. Once again, he felt a slight jolt of contact as he took her elbow and helped her from the car, then led her down the sidewalk. Somewhere in the distance he could hear music and the faint sound of a crowd.

"I'll try eating first."

This time when she slid her arm through the crook of his elbow, the action was more practiced, more familiar. Jack led her down a narrow flight of stairs to a dimly lit restaurant. Steam had clouded the glass of the multipaned door, and when he and Eleanor entered, they were immediately surrounded by the rich smells of marinara sauce, fresh bread and spices.

A waitress led them to a secluded table in the corner, and Jack helped Eleanor remove her coat and settle in her chair. Then he took his own seat.

"Would you like me to read the menu?" he asked.

"Please."

He reviewed the list of soups, salads and pastas available, as well as the choices of specialty dishes. By that time the waitress appeared, and both of them quickly ordered. The heady aromas were making Jack conscious of his own hunger, and he could imagine that Eleanor felt much the same way. Therefore, it was a relief when the waitress returned with a tureen of minestrone soup and a fat loaf of bread, thus alleviating the need for small talk.

The fact that he found the silence uncomfortable surprised Jack. He'd had enough blind dates and set-ups that he shouldn't feel the need to fill every moment with sound. But with each second in Eleanor's company he found himself aware of how he relied upon visual cues to express himself. He wasn't generally a talker, so to find himself thrust into a position of being the dominant conversationalist was unnerving.

"You've grown quiet," Eleanor stated.

"I figured I should give you a chance to eat."

"Ahh."

He didn't like the way she drawled in response, as if she knew what was racing through his mind.

"In that case, is there some Parmesan on the table?"

He handed her the oversize shaker, becoming aware of the satiny texture of her skin when their fingers brushed. Then the contact was broken.

Knowing he needed to get hold of his own wayward musings, he asked, "So how did you get to be a textbook advisor for the university?"

He noted that way her lips momentarily tightened. "I'm sure my father had something to do with it. He's the dean of education."

"You don't approve of his actions, I take it?"

"I dislike being the object of—" She clamped her mouth shut before she could say the words. Charity. Pity. She needn't have bothered to censor her reaction, he knew what she'd been about to say.

"How do you know he had ulterior motives in suggesting your name for the job? Maybe he and the other deans were playing a round of golf, and the dean of art, or whatever he is, said, 'Hey, I need someone to give me an opinion on some really boring books.' Your father was probably the only one who volunteered a name."

Her lips trembled at the corners from her effort to control an unwilling smile.

"Perhaps you're right."

He allowed her to eat for a few minutes, then could not temper his need to know more, to find out everything he could about Eleanor Rappaport.

"So what do you do during the day?"

"I work at a theater."

"Legitimate?" he asked, although he already

knew she didn't work on the stage, but in a movie house.

"Film."

"Ahh. Now you're talking my language."

"Hardly. I stock the candy counter and help take tickets."

"Do you enjoy it?"

Her shoulders lifted in a faint shrug. "It's a good job."

He felt a twinge of guilt. "But it's not what you want to be doing."

Her fork poked at the pasta on her plate. "I was an artist before the accident."

"What sort of art did you do?"

"Murals, mostly."

"No kidding? I'm impressed. Have I seen any of your stuff?"

"I've got a wall at the Phoenix Civic Center, ceilings at five state capitals, subway murals in New York and Washington, D.C., several schools, shopping malls, business complexes and parks all over the country."

"You must have been good."

He saw the pain that settled over her features before she dropped a mask of unconcern over her features.

"I was."

The statement was filled with confidence and regret.

"So what are you doing with your art now?"

Her brow creased. "It's a little difficult to paint when you can't see what you're doing."

"But surely you've been trained in other forms?"

"I took a quarter of sculpture in college."

"So why aren't you sculpting?"

"It isn't that easy to transfer mediums, you know."

"Nor is it impossible."

She reached for the wineglass that the waitress had just filled.

"Can we talk about something else?"

"Why?"

She sighed. "My art wasn't something I willingly gave up. It was something that was stolen from me." Her anger was evident. "It's taken me a long time to accept the fact. Now that I have, I don't wish to dwell on my limitations."

"But according to your landladies, your limitations are only temporary."

"They've been gossiping again," she murmured.

"No, they're just concerned. To be honest, they're worried about a woman who'll be raising a child out of wedlock."

She gasped. "They didn't say that, did they?"

"I think they wanted to shock me with your liberated attitude."

"And were you shocked?"

It was clear that she held her breath slightly as she waited for his answer.

"No. In fact, I was a little…relieved."

"Relieved."

"If the baby's father is out of the picture, I don't have to worry about the proud papa showing up and pounding me into the ground for taking you to dinner.''

Her lips twitched at his teasing remark, but he wondered what she would say if he confessed that his words held a grain of truth.

Not wanting her to guess the full import of his interest, he said, ''According to Minnie, you're considering eye surgery once the baby is born.''

''Yes, but the surgery is a gamble. I may only enjoy a partial return of my sight.''

''As a sculptor, you could channel your energies elsewhere and—''

''So tell me about yourself, Jack,'' she interrupted sternly.

Jack fought the urge to chuckle in delight. Eleanor was so intent on changing the subject that she was willing to risk offending him—something he sensed was atypical of her nature. Nevertheless, he let her have her way. Not because he was ready to drop the subject completely, but because he sensed a germ of an idea had been planted in her head, and he should give her time to grow accustomed to it.

''What do you want to know about me? My life is completely boring.''

''You jump off buildings.''

''Someone has to do it.''

'But why do *you* do it?''

''Because I'm paid disgusting amounts of money to do so.''

''So you're rich?''

''Hardly. But I can afford to pick and choose my assignments.''

"I don't think any amount of money could induce me to jump off a building."

"Why? You wouldn't see the ground rushing up to meet you."

This time *she* laughed—and he was grateful. He didn't want her to think he was mocking her in any way, but neither did he want her to think that her blindness made him uncomfortable. He was often disturbed by Eleanor, intrigued, enchanted, but those emotions had nothing to do with her sightlessness. Rather, he was enamored by the woman herself. By her beauty and iron will she displayed time and time again.

"I've heard it said that thrill seekers are subconsciously seeking death." Her own teasing rejoinder held a daring note, and he reached out to take her hand.

"I prefer to look at it as risking life."

"What do you mean?"

"In order to enjoy living, sometimes you have to appreciate how dear such a gift can be. There's nothing in this world that can compare to standing at the edge of a cliff, having your heart pound, your mind freeze on a single objective."

He felt her shudder.

"I think I'd rather live in ignorance of such nuances, thank you very much."

Jack couldn't help himself. His thumb stroked her knuckles, absorbing their resiliency, their fragility.

"Although..." she continued.

"What?"

"There was a time a few years ago when I was tempted to try skydiving. Just once."

"Did you do it?"

She shook her head. "No. Somehow, I never found the time or the emotional fortitude."

"You should do it someday."

"No. I don't think so."

"Why not?"

"It wouldn't be nearly so enjoyable now. I wouldn't be able to 'see the ground rush up to meet me,'" she quipped.

Her tone was light, but he caught the hint of regret.

"You never know. It might be an even more thrilling adventure."

Deftly she wriggled her hand loose. "Not for me, I'm afraid. Besides, the art department would never forgive me if I died before I had a chance to finish all their textbook evaluations."

Jack knew that as far as she was concerned, the subject was closed. He allowed her to return to her food without interruption—Eleanor was so caught up in the restrictions of her blindness that she couldn't seem to redirect her energies. He found himself tempted to help her widen her scope and teach her to take chances.

He shook his head. The whole situation was absurd. His accident must have damaged his brain more than anyone had originally thought. What other reason could he have for meddling in another person's private life.

Chapter Seven

When they emerged from the restaurant, Jack paused, and Eleanor's fingers automatically tightened around his arm.

"What's wrong?" she asked, listening more intently to the noises around them.

"A crowd has developed on the sidewalk."

She tipped her head, noting the distant thumping of rock music, laughter and conversation.

"We must be near Larimer Square."

"How did you know?"

She laughed at his obvious incredulity. "I work nearby. A craft fair will be here for the rest of the week, and the local bars and restaurants are using the event as a reason to host a party."

Jack placed his free hand over the fingers crooked around his arm. The action was completely ordinary—hadn't her mother done the same thing hundreds of times? But when Jack completed the gesture, she found her body warming in a way it had never done before. His fingers were long and thin, callused yet infinitely appealing. She could imagine how any woman would enjoy having them stroke down her—

Stop it!

"How's your headache?"

"What?" Eleanor gasped, yanking her thoughts into line.

"Your headache."

Eleanor smiled when she realized the dull pounding had disappeared. "It's gone."

The moment she gave her answer she realized she may have made a tactical error. After all, she had the perfect excuse to go home and send Jack on his way. But for some reason she found herself loath to do such a thing. As much as this man disturbed her, it had been a long time since she'd had the opportunity to get out of her apartment.

She felt his thumb rub over her knuckles. "Do you have enough energy to investigate the fair?"

The good food and wine had chased away her weariness, but she didn't immediately respond. She wanted to investigate the gathering—more than she would have thought possible. But even as she considered accepting the invitation, she became abruptly conscious of the number of people who must have thronged to the area. Eleanor had managed to learn how to get around on her own, but she still wasn't comfortable in large groups. If she decided to allow Jack to lead her into the crowds, she would have to rely on him completely.

She would have to trust him.

She'd never been much good with trust. At least that's what Roger had said. He'd claimed she was a

control freak—and even though she hadn't con-
curred with his snap diagnosis of her psyche, she
did have to admit she liked to be prepared for all
contingencies.

"Come on, Eleanor. Say yes."

Jack's voice slid into the darkness in her head,
brushing against her senses like the stroke of a vel-
vet glove.

"I promise to hold on to you. I won't let you trip
or make a spectacle of yourself."

Eleanor supposed she should have been offended
at his offhand remarks, but his blunt remark caused
her to laugh. "Thanks so much for your vote of
confidence."

"Besides, all the good food has given you a natural buzz."

That fact was true, but she doubted her heightened
senses had anything to do with a full stomach. She
was more sure that this man had something to do
with her current state. Throughout the entire evening
he'd been charming and attentive. He hadn't
dwelled on her blindness as some people were prone
to do, nor did he ignore it completely. Instead, he
treated her condition as if it held no more import
than being slightly nearsighted.

Even so, she preferred to keep their relationship
completely businesslike. Professional.

Staid.

Dull.

Drat, why did she have to analyze every aspect
of her existence? Why did she have to worry what

consequences might arrive from this evening? Why couldn't she give herself up to the moment?

Because you're about to become a mother and you can't afford to let your life grow any more complicated than it already is.

"Give me an hour," Jack murmured next to her ear, bending so close that his breath tickled the delicate hairs and warmed her skin.

"We have books to read," she insisted, but her voice emerged far too weak to be any sort of deterrent.

"They will still be there when we get back."

True enough.

"Okay," she relented, wondering what had possessed her to even consider the outing. "But if I say I've had enough—"

"Then we're on our way back to your apartment."

Her hand curled more securely around his elbow, offering her tacit acceptance of the plan.

They made their way up the staircase to ground level, then began walking closer and closer to the source of the noise. The sidewalks were crowded with raucous humanity who seemed not at all discouraged by the recent rainy weather. Within minutes Eleanor could tell by the circuitous route they were taking that stalls loaded with wares had been planted in every available space. She could hear conversations about hand-mixed perfumes, bird houses, caricatures and hats. Somewhere to her left it sounded as if a puppet show was in progress, and to her right the jingling of store bells signified that people were being drawn into the shops, as well.

"Maybe we should have eaten here," Jack commented at the same moment the heavenly smell of braised meat and beer wafted her way.

"I don't think anything could top the Italian food we had at Gionelli's."

"You're probably right, but I'm all in favor of working up some room for dessert."

She cocked her head, trying to discern the myriad smells. "Why? What's caught your attention?"

"Candied apples. Huge gooey ones covered in caramel or chocolate or red syrup. I haven't seen anything like those since I was a kid and my grandmother made them for Halloween."

"Is she still alive?"

"Gran?"

"Mmm-hmm."

"You bet. She's on a cruise right now—Martinique, I think."

The driving rhythm of a reggae band slid through the din, and Eleanor turned her head in that direction.

"Would you like to go closer?" Jack asked.

"Sure."

They moved a few dozen steps, and the melody grew louder and more intoxicating. When they stopped, Eleanor realized they must be standing next to a small dance floor. She could hear the rustle of clothing and the scraping of feet.

"Would you like to dance?"

She immediately shook her head, then hoped her

reaction didn't appear as panicked as she felt. It had been years since she'd danced in any way or fashion, and she didn't feel like making a spectacle of herself—a fear that had nothing to do with her blindness or her pregnancy.

Besides which, she added silently to herself, it wouldn't be a good idea for her to dance with Jack. Dancing implied…intimacy. And that was one emotion she didn't want to encourage. It was hard enough remembering that the two of them had a job to fulfill. One that didn't include cozy dinners and street festivals.

The band came to a rousing finish and immediately segued into a slow ballad.

"Come on," Jack murmured silkily. "This is a nice slow one."

Before she had the presence of mind to protest, he drew her into his arms and pulled her onto the dance floor.

Eleanor immediately froze, her mind scrambling to remember the social dancing course she'd taken as a freshman in college. She soon realized she had very little to worry about. Jack had drawn her close to his body, and other than a slight sway from side to side, he didn't require fancy footwork on her part.

"That's not so bad, is it?" he murmured.

Eleanor wasn't sure how she should respond to his question. If she said no, Jack would take her answer as encouragement, but if she said yes, she'd be lying. Standing in the embrace of this man was far from horrible. It was comforting and disturbing and exhilarating all at once.

Luckily Jack didn't seem to require an answer. He drew her even closer, linking his hands behind her back and bending to rest his head near hers.

Her eyes closed—in pleasure, in regret. So many months had passed since a man had held her. Being held this way made her remember the headiness of falling in love, the delight to be found in sharing time with someone you adored. This was the very reason why she hadn't mourned Roger's desertion for more than a few weeks. She had known that if she couldn't have love, real love, then she didn't want second best.

But now the die was cast. And just when she was on the precipice of a possible relationship, she was already expecting a child. She couldn't help thinking that if she and Jack—

Whoa.

She shouldn't even be considering such things. Not with any man. Right now her life had enough upheaval of its own. She didn't need to court more. She had so many things to do, so many duties.

Like what? Decorating a nursery she had heretofore avoided? Stocking the candy counter at The Flick?

Abruptly she stepped away. "I'd like to go home now."

She knew her request took him by surprise. There was a beat of unanswered silence, then, "Sure. If that's what you want."

Eleanor had expected an argument, but Jack kept his promise, leading her back to the car in complete silence. After driving the short distance to her home, he helped Eleanor from the car as if they were a pair of teenagers returning from a date and her mother was watching from the window. He was so polite, so solicitous, so…distant, that she nearly—*nearly*—regretted ending their evening.

But she had to end it. She had to get away from him. She needed space and some time to gather her composure and decide what she wanted to do.

What she wanted to do? a voice in her head mocked. *Do you really want to think? You want him to touch you.*

Stop it!

Eleanor waited until they'd reached the stoop before saying, "Listen, I'm sorry, but my headache is coming back, and I think I'd rather skip our reading session, if you don't mind."

He didn't immediately answer, and she prayed he wouldn't call her bluff.

"When would you like to meet again?" he finally asked when the silence threatened to go on too long.

"Tomorrow will be fine."

"I'll meet you at the same time, then."

Meaning what? That he would be early for their appointment?

But she didn't ask. Not when it was taking most of the control she possessed not to ask him to stay. Knowing her restraint was limited, she said, "Great. I'll expect you then."

She held out her hand for him to shake, not knowing why she offered the gesture, but feeling driven to make things seem completely casual between them.

"Until tomorrow, Jack."

His hand swallowed hers, enclosing her fingers in a grip that was warm and strong and masculine. But when she would have released him, he did not let go.

"Is anything wrong?" he asked, his voice a mere thread of sound in the evening stillness.

Eleanor felt him leaning toward her. Instinctively she knew his head had bent and was...

Within kissing distance.

"Wrong?" she breathed. Did he suspect? Did he know that she wanted him to kiss her? More than she had wanted anything in a long time? Could he possibly suspect that she was, in essence, running away from what he made her think and feel? "What could possibly be wrong?" she said, bluffing.

"I don't know. You seemed to be enjoying yourself at the fair."

"I was."

"But when we started dancing, you were ready to come home."

"I...I just..." She scrambled for an explanation that didn't make her sound as adolescent as she was feeling. "All the noise just brought my headache back, that's all."

She could feel the warmth of his breath against her cheek. It would have been so easy to lift on tiptoes and...

"So I haven't offended you?" he asked.

"No. Not at all."

"Good."

She swallowed against the dryness in her throat

when he caressed the back of her hand with his thumb. The gesture was becoming his trademark in her own mind. Those soft touches. That deep voice.

Not for the first time that evening she wished she could see him, wished she could read his expression. He'd said his eyes were brown, but she would have done anything to have seen them at that moment. Had they grown dark and molten with the same awareness thrumming through her own body? Or was he merely being friendly?

She shivered when the backs of his fingers touched her cheek, stroking from her temple to her chin.

"You're a beautiful woman, Eleanor Rappaport."

His voice was a mere whisper, and her soul expanded with every word.

"Do you know what you do to me?"

She wasn't sure if he'd actually made the comment aloud or if she'd dreamed it. In either case, when he backed away from her, she felt bereft.

"I'll see you tomorrow then."

"Sure."

Sure? Couldn't she have thought of anything more scintillating to say?

Such as what? *Kiss me. Kiss me now?*

In an instant Jack was gone, his footsteps retreating to the curb. Eleanor heard the slam of his door, the roar of his engine, the hiss of tires on the wet street. Then, the silence closed around her, making her feel unaccountably alone and...

Anxious.

Anxious for tomorrow. For what the next encounter with Jack might bring.

"HI, MOM," Eleanor called as she entered her mother's boutique and the brass bell overhead tinkled.

"Eleanor! What a surprise! I'm just finishing a customer layaway, then I'll be right with you."

"Take your time. I'm in no hurry."

Eleanor made her way through the familiar shop to the counter at the rear of the store, where she quickly located her mother's high stool. Perching on top, she idly listened to her mother's prattle and the customer's response.

As the minutes ticked past, Eleanor wondered what she was doing in Victoria's Closet. She had no need of clothes—certainly none of the romantic creations her mother stocked. She should stick to standard maternity wear: jeans and sweaters and T-shirts.

But even though Eleanor had told herself the same thing a half dozen times, she was still here. And before she left, she knew she would have a new ensemble. Maybe the onset of spring was infecting her system, or maybe it was the burst of warm weather they'd had that day. Whatever the reason, she wanted something new and light and different.

"Now, how can I help you, dear?"

She heard the jingle of her mother's jewelry as Regina approached, then the whisper-soft caress of her mother's fingers as she swept a lock of hair from Eleanor's brow.

"I was just in the mood for some new clothes. I knew you'd kill me if I went to the competition."

She waited, hoping her mother would take her answer at face value.

"What's the occasion?"

"Occasion?" Eleanor echoed, thinking quickly. "Why does there have to be an occasion?"

Her mother chuckled. "When a pregnant woman buys something new to wear, there is *always* an occasion—whether it be real or imagined—and ninety percent of the time, the occasion has something to do with a man."

Eleanor nearly cursed aloud when she felt a betraying heat rise in her cheeks.

Her mother clapped her hands in delight. "Is that it? Are you seeing someone?"

"No, Mother."

"Well, you should. My little grandchild will be here soon, and it's already past time you resurrected your social life."

Eleanor resisted the urge to roll her eyes. Her mother had always been under the impression that, being an artist, her daughter had enjoyed a bohemian life-style. She'd never accepted the fact that Eleanor didn't have hordes of men trying to beat down her door.

"I hardly think that *resurrect* is the proper term to use in this instance, Mother."

"Then you haven't been paying attention. I can't even remember the last time you went out for a night on the town."

Last night. With Jack.

"Is he someone worth impressing?" her mother asked.

"Who?"

"The man who put the twinkle in your eyes."

"Mo-ther," Eleanor groaned. "I hardly think my eyes twinkle."

"If you only knew. Now, who are we trying to impress?"

Eleanor sighed. "*We* are not trying to impress anyone. I would merely like to have something new to wear."

"And who will be seeing you in this new creation?"

Eleanor wriggled slightly in her seat. She should have known that Regina Rappaport—interrogator extraordinaire—would expect a debriefing on everything that had occurred in Eleanor's life in the past few days. Especially any details that might remotely relate to a man.

"The only person who might see me in my new clothes would be my reader."

"Your reader?" Her mother sounded clearly disappointed.

"Yes."

"What's her name?"

Eleanor hesitated, wishing there were some way to avoid explaining that her reader wasn't a woman.

"Well, what's her name?"

Eleanor took a breath, then exhaled and hurriedly said, "His name is Jack," hoping her mother would miss part of the information in the rush of air.

She should have known better.

"*His* name is Jack!" Regina clapped her hands again in delight. "When are you seeing him next?"

"Tonight," Eleanor admitted uneasily.

"Then we don't have a minute to lose! I'm so glad I decided to diversify into some maternity things last year."

Within minutes Eleanor found herself ensconced in a dressing room while her mother thrust hangers at her.

"This is a glorious chiffon number—empire waist, sleeveless, scoop neck."

"Sleeveless?" Eleanor protested. "Yesterday we hit a high of fifty degrees."

"But today we hit sixty-five!" her mother insisted. "Besides, I've got a *marvelous* cropped sweater you can wear with it."

"What color is it?"

"Pink."

Eleanor moaned. "You know I hate pink."

"But it brings out the color of your cheeks."

Not a selling point to Eleanor since she always felt flushed when Jack was near.

"Next," Eleanor pronounced, extending the hanger through the half-open door.

Her mother sighed, handing her another garment. "This is a beautiful *blue* print organza."

"Organza? I'm not going to the prom."

"You might need something another night that's a bit dressy, and I—"

"Next."

"Try this one, then."

"What is it?"

"A simple hand-embroidered blouse with a high yoke and softly gathered sleeves."

"How simple?"

"Very simple."

"I don't want to look like a tourist who's just stepped off the boat from Mazatlan."

"You won't look like a tourist. It looks more…antiquey than touristy."

"What color?"

"Ivory. You can wear it with these wonderful silk slacks."

"Silk?"

"A very chic brushed silk, taupe colored."

Eleanor took the proffered items and closed the door. Within seconds she'd donned the clothes and, at least in her opinion, thought they were just what she needed. The fabrics were elegant to the touch, the tailoring simple, yet tasteful.

"How do they look?" she asked opening the door.

"Wonderful!"

"You're sure?"

"Of course I'm sure. Do you think I'd allow my daughter to buy something that made her look like an orphan?"

No. Regina wouldn't. But only because Eleanor's mother took great pride in her store and her daughter. Otherwise she would probably be as indulgent with Eleanor's wardrobe as she was ensuring her daughter ate well and slept well.

"I'll take it."

"Good. I've got a few more pieces for you to try on."

"This is all I need, Mother."

"Nonsense. You'll need something for going out."

"Mother, I told you Jack was my reader. We won't be going out."

But they'd already gone out. To dinner and the fair. And he'd been on the verge of kissing her. She *knew* he'd been on the verge of kissing her.

"Nevertheless, you need a few more things. In case you and your reader go somewhere…public to study."

Eleanor bit her lip to keep from laughing but didn't protest. After all, it had been quite some time since she'd indulged in pretty clothes rather than a strictly utilitarian wardrobe. Why not surrender to the temptation while she was still in the mood?

Especially since she might, just might, say yes if Jack asked her out again.

Chapter Eight

Jack waited on a park bench across from Victoria's Closet. Watching. Wondering what in hell had made him come here today.

But he knew the answer as soon as the question flashed through his mind. Eleanor. He worried about her—far more than he should. He'd known her only a few days, and already he found himself consumed with whether she was eating right, sleeping right. What preparations had she made for the baby? What dreams had she abandoned? Who did she turn to when she was lonely?

From there he found himself remembering how she looked, the scent of her hair, the silken texture of her skin. He found himself wondering how she would have reacted if he'd kissed her last night. He'd wanted to kiss her so badly. And by resisting the temptation he'd doomed himself to dreams of Eleanor and him, a romantic retreat, twisted sheets, and...

No!

Jack brought a hand to his face and rubbed at the

ache across his brow. Not for the first time he tried
to convince himself that he had no business thinking
such thoughts. But after holding her close as they'd
danced and inhaling the fragrance of her hair, it was
natural that his sleep had been filled with her image.

Jack's hand shook ever so slightly as he lifted a
carton of chocolate milk to his lips.

Yes, he was definitely losing his mind, he thought
as he watched Eleanor emerge from her mother's
shop. He needed to keep a professional, nonemo-
tional, completely neutral attitude about this woman.

But in an instant he knew he was in trouble. She
was wearing a dress. A loose, filmy dress that
swayed around her long legs, cupped the roundness
of her breasts and highlighted the beautiful blush
that tinged her cheeks.

And somehow Jack knew he was the inspiration
for that blush.

JACK WASN'T WAITING on her stoop when Eleanor
arrived home, and Eleanor found herself strangely
disappointed. She'd grown so used to having him
anticipate her movements that she was beginning to
accept the way he seemed one step ahead of her—
both physically and emotionally.

A dangerous attitude.

Very dangerous indeed.

Letting herself into her apartment, she hurried into
the bedroom, throwing the sacks from her mother's
boutique onto the bed. If she had time she would
put them away before Jack came, but right now it

was more important that she comb her hair and freshen her makeup.

When the doorbell rang a few minutes later, Eleanor had tied her thick tresses at the back with a ribbon, applied a light sheen of lipstick and a dusting of blush and eye shadow.

As her fingers closed around the doorknob, she found her heart pounding in a strange way. What would Jack say about her hair? Her new dress? Surely he would approve. After all, he'd been the one to suggest that she adopt a less formal attitude.

The hinges squeaked slightly as Eleanor opened the door. For a moment she envisioned the way Jack must look as he stood in front of her. She did her best to make the angles and planes of his face take a three-dimension form in her mind. She could all but feel the way he'd braced his hands against the jamb and leaned forward ever so slightly.

The air between them suddenly crackled with a potent energy. One that made her realize she wasn't alone in her feelings of expectation.

"Hi."

She felt a part of her melt into a drippy puddle of need. The single-word greeting Jack had used held a host of emotions. Pleasure, wariness and warmth.

"Hi, yourself."

Was that really her voice? She sounded so coy, so flirtatious.

"Ready to read?"

"Of course." She held the door wide. "Come on in."

She waited until he'd brushed past her, leaving a waft of his familiar woodsy cologne. Then she closed the door and made her way to the chair opposite the couch. Touching the back with her fingers, she asked, "Can I get you something? A drink? A snack?"

"A drink would be great. Thanks."

She heard the zip of his jacket and imagined what it must be. Leather, she would think. Jack struck her as the type who would wear leather.

"Beer?"

"Sure."

She took a beer from the refrigerator for Jack and a mineral water for herself, then poured some pretzels into a shallow bowl before making her way back to the living room. After setting the refreshments on the steamer trunk that doubled as a coffee table, she sat in the chair, drawing her feet beneath her and tucking the ends of her skirt beneath her legs.

"That's a beautiful dress."

The comment warmed her, and she relaxed even more.

He'd noticed. As unreasonable as her thoughts had been, she'd been so worried that all of her preparations with her mother might have been for naught.

"Thank you."

"It's new, isn't it?"

"Yes."

"I like it. That shade of yellow is very nice against your skin."

He was offering her more compliments than she had even dared to hope for, and the effect was electrifying. She found herself emboldened in a way she would never have thought possible.

"Describe the color."

She knew. Her mother had already informed her that the dress was pale-yellow with sprigs of fresh spring flowers, but she wanted to know how a man would describe it. How *this* man would describe it.

"It's yellow."

"I know it's yellow," she said with a grin. "But what color of yellow?"

A silence settled around them. Then he said, "It's the color of banana pudding."

She laughed. What had she expected? Some romantic, poetic description?

"Is something wrong?" he asked.

"No. Nothing." But she couldn't prevent her grin.

"You're sure?"

"Yes."

"Because I would feel terrible if you had some aversion to banana pudding," he said.

"Not really—although it brings to mind grandmothers and hand-knit sweaters."

"Trust me. You don't look like a grandmother."

The words stroked her with their silken tone.

"You don't look like a grandmother at all," he repeated more emphatically.

The couch springs creaked. She felt his hand against her cheek and knew he must have knelt in front of her.

"What are you doing to me, Eleanor?"

The question was so unexpected she couldn't respond.

"Sometimes when I'm with you, I think that I'm losing my sanity."

She frowned at his remark. "Why?"

His caress grew more insistent, more demanding. His thumb slid down her throat, then his fingers cupped the back of her skull.

"None of this was supposed to be complicated. I met you intending to do a job. I would be your reader, but nothing else."

A rush of gooseflesh rippled down her spine.

"But each time I'm with you, I find it harder and harder to remember I'm merely a volunteer."

Eleanor licked her lips to ease their dryness.

"Don't do that," he rasped.

"What?"

"Don't lick your lips. Don't tempt me any more than I've already been tempted. If you do, I won't be able to stop myself."

"Do you want to stop yourself?"

She heard his sharp intake of breath.

"No," he said firmly. "I don't."

Then his lips covered hers in a searing kiss, and her own arms were winding around his shoulders, pulling him closer—even as a voice of warning reverberated in her head.

Don't do this. Not now. Not while you are so vulnerable.

Eleanor ignored the words of caution. She was tired of being vulnerable, tired of being cautious.

She didn't want to remember that this man was a temporary element of her life. She didn't want to remember that he had a job she feared and a lifestyle she knew nothing about. All she wanted was this moment. This kiss.

Her arms tightened around his neck, and she found herself being lifted toward him, into him, her body colliding with his chest.

His hands swept down her spine, crushing her against his hard, athletic length. His tongue pressed for entrance and she let him in to explore her moist softness. He tasted of beer and salt and man, and to Eleanor the effect was too heady to endure.

She shuddered when she felt one of his hands slipping down, down, his fingers bunching the fabric of her dress, lifting the hem higher and higher until he encountered her hot, bare flesh.

Breaking away from her, he tipped his head back, sucking a huge breath into his lungs and holding it there. When finally he released the air again, she found herself staring as hard as she could at his face, wishing that she could pierce the darkness. Just once. She needed to know what he was thinking and feeling.

Automatically her fingers spread wide over his cheeks, searching out the planes and angles of his face. She felt a definite tension in the areas she explored, a blatant intensity. But the exploration wasn't enough. She needed to get inside him. She needed him to tell her the things she couldn't see.

"Come on."

He stood abruptly, helping her to plant her feet securely on the carpet again.

"Where are we—"

"To a party."

"A party?" she gasped, hurt. She'd been shaken to the core by his kiss. She had been ready to open her soul to him. Had he felt nothing more than the need for some sort of entertainment?

Her thoughts must have paraded across her face, because he framed her cheeks in his hands.

"I've got to take you someplace public."

"Why?"

"Because if I don't, I'm going to be kissing you again, caressing you."

Eleanor's body became hot and needy at the mere words.

"I see."

Her response was weak and ineffective, but he didn't seem to notice, because he continued without pausing.

"If that occurs, I won't be responsible for what could happen next."

"What do you think would happen?"

His fingers dug into her scalp. "Surely you're not that naive." He drew her closer. So close that she couldn't ignore the blatant heat of his own body and the evidence of his arousal. "I assume you have a bedroom somewhere down that hall?"

His query thrilled her.

Aroused her.

Frightened her.

"Yes." She had to force the word past a throat grown tight with nerves and excitement.

"Then I think it would be a good idea if we avoided it this evening, don't you?"

He didn't wait for her answer. Taking her hand, he twined their fingers together and drew her after him.

"So we're going to a party," he announced. "Maybe after some noise and music and laughter, we can forget this all happened and come back here to get some work done."

Eleanor frowned, balking at his last remark.

Forget? He wanted to forget their kiss? Their embrace?

"Is that what you want? To ignore everything that happened and move on as if it never occurred?" She made a waving gesture with her free hand to indicate the passionate exchange they'd shared.

Jack tugged on her hand, forcing her to stumble against his chest. Then he wrapped her close to his body.

"I don't want to forget anything." His voice was rough and filled with desire.

Then he was kissing her again, making her entirely conscious of his true feelings.

Standing on tiptoe, she leaned into him, allowing herself to feel the rush of desire that threatened to inundate her senses. Distantly a part of her prayed she wasn't making a mistake. Since her accident and Roger's desertion, she'd been so careful with her emotions. She'd remained guarded and wary with anyone outside her family. Yet here she was, opening her heart up to a stranger.

She could be hurt.

But if she sent him away, she would never know where these feelings might lead her. She would never know how much this man could have offered her, body and soul. Already he'd awakened a part of her that had been dormant far too long. She needed him. Needed the vitality he offered her. If she refused this opportunity, she knew she would never be able to forgive herself.

Jack released her abruptly. They were both breathing hard, and the sound was comforting to her. Comforting and very envigorating.

She'd disturbed him. This man—this strong, indomitable man who jumped from buildings for a living—had been unnerved by her response to his kiss. The very notion filled her with a potent sense of power and femininity as well as an unshakable confidence.

"Do you want a sweater or something?" His voice sounded sandpaper rough.

Eleanor yanked her own thoughts into line, but it was difficult to assimilate such a mundane question when her body thrummed with pent-up sexual energy.

"No. I don't need a sweater."

"You're sure? It's chilly when the wind blows."

"If the weather turns cold, I'll borrow your jacket."

Her statement was bold, indicating that she felt he would concede to such a request—and, even more important, that she felt in a position to make such a demand.

"Fine."

In one word he had accepted her challenge. He had allowed her to mark him as a date. Not a business associate. Not a reader. But a date. A companion.

A partner.

His arm slid around her waist, and he drew her into the crook of his body. The move was completely calculated. He, too, was making demands on this relationship.

Eleanor moved willingly into the embrace, wondering how things could change so quickly and yet so slowly. Just yesterday she had worried about putting her reader in his place. Tonight they had tacitly agreed to allow the partnership to become much more personal.

"Let's go," Jack said, his voice rich with intimate nuance.

"Just lead the way."

JACK HEARD the deep *bump, bump, bump* of a bass guitar and felt the vibrations echo in the ground beneath him long before he reached the door to Victor's apartment.

"It'll be loud," he warned, his fingers tightening around Eleanor's.

"I think I can stand it."

"If we get separated, don't panic. I'll find you."

"Fine."

But he could tell by the slight quaver in her voice

that she was nervous about joining his friends. Strangers. All of them.

The music intensified the moment the door opened. Eleanor instinctively stiffened, but he didn't allow her to draw back too far. Slipping his arm around her waist, he ushered her into the apartment and through the hoards of people who occupied every available space.

At first Eleanor kept close to his side. Not clinging, no. Her grip was firm but by no means desperate. Outwardly she looked calm and cool and collected.

But inwardly he knew she had some misgivings about the evening. Except for the craft fair, she probably hadn't been in such a large group of people for some time—and a part of him wanted to make sure she had a good time. So much so, that he steered her toward those of his contemporaries he knew would draw her out.

Soon she was conversing about a museum exhibit with an artistic director who, Jack vaguely remembered, had lived in New Jersey a few years back. Jack was even able to slip away from her side to freshen their drinks. When he returned and she smiled he knew he'd done the right thing in bringing her here tonight.

Grinning, he stepped close to her, so close that her back rested against his chest. When his arm slid around her rounded stomach, she leaned against him, the movement so easy and natural that he could scarcely believe they'd known each other less than a week. Bending, he brushed his lips against the top of her head, needing to touch her, draw her close, catch a whiff of the sweet scent that clung to her hair.

From time to time he caught the curious glances of his associates, especially Victor. He knew that they'd never seen him with a date, let alone someone as refined and high-class as Eleanor Rappaport. He knew they were dying to know why he was dating a pregnant woman. There were bound to be questions about how serious the relationship was.

How serious was it?

The thought raced through his consciousness, tarnishing the bright glow of the evening and forcing him to look hard at his own motives. What *did* Jack intend to do now that he'd insinuated himself into Eleanor's life?

He frowned, the conversation flowing around him like the rhythm of a distant tide.

He was attracted to Eleanor, there was no denying that point. In fact, *attraction* seemed like much too mild a word to explain what she inspired in him. Sometimes he found himself irritated by her stubborn pride, at others he was in awe of her natural courage. Then she would look up at him with those large, sightless eyes and make him forget everything but hauling her into his arms—a fact that probably made him some sort of a sicko.

In any event, there was no easy way to proceed. In the past he'd known from the beginning what to expect from the women he pursued—and in many ways he'd known exactly how their liaisons would end. Either filming would end or a new project would begin and Jack would relocate for several months, offering a natural termination of his affections.

Jack's arm wound even tighter around Eleanor's waist, and he breathed deeply of her heady perfume. Then a tiny pressure moved against his hand and he froze.

The baby. The baby had kicked him.

He swallowed hard, cursing himself for complicating Eleanor's life even more. She'd suffered so many disappointments and challenges during the past few months, and with a baby on the way, the last thing she needed was someone like him in her life.

But he already knew that leaving this woman would not be easy. She needed him. She didn't know it yet, but she needed him more than she'd ever needed anyone else. Not as a reader but as a friend.

A lover.

He wanted to draw her out of her self-imposed withdrawal and show her that she had so much to offer the world—and not behind a candy counter at a theater.

The vehemence of his thoughts surprised him. As he gazed around the room, crowded with actors and grips and lighting technicians, he admitted that in meeting this woman his own focus had changed. In analyzing Eleanor's predicament, he'd been forced to look at his own. And what he found wasn't pleasant.

He'd become a lonely, self-absorbed man im-

mersed in his work to the exclusion of all other re-
lationships. He realized that he knew most of the
guests at the party, had worked with some of them
more than once, but had never formed any real
friendships with them. Even One-Eye and Victor
Russo were little more than business associates.

"Is something wrong?"

Eleanor's voice pierced the haze of his thoughts,
and he started.

"Wrong?"

She touched his wrist, her fingers slender and delicate and feminine. "You became suddenly tense. I
thought you were trying to squeeze the air from my
lungs."

Jack winced when he realized how tightly he'd
been holding her. "Sorry."

"Don't be. Not tonight. I've been having a wonderful time."

He bent to kiss her cheek. "I'm glad."

"Is that dancing I hear in the corner?"

He glanced in the direction she indicated, noting
that a half dozen couples had begun to sway to the
music blasting from the sound equipment.

"It appears to be."

"Wanna dance?" she asked, her expression pos-
itively wicked.

"Why?" he asked suspiciously, even as he drew
her through the clumps of people.

"We never really had a chance to finish the dance
we started yesterday evening."

"No. We didn't."

"So…" she drawled, stepping into his arms. "Impress me with your skill."

He smiled, drawing her close and pushing his own disquieting thoughts to the back of his mind.

"Your wish is my command."

Chapter Nine

She'd had a good time, Eleanor thought late the next morning when Jack finally left her to get some sleep. Dawn had long since come and gone and they'd spent the night cuddled up together on the couch.

Eleanor's eyes closed briefly and she touched her lips with her fingertips.

No. She'd had a *wonderful* time.

Leaning her back against the door, she smiled happily to herself, her body still radiating with the pleasure of Jack's kisses. Until now she hadn't known how much she'd missed by leading such a solitary existence. She hadn't been to a party in ages, hadn't danced, hadn't bantered with strangers.

Then Jack had stormed into her life and forced her to reexamine everything she did.

Laughing softly to herself, she realized they still hadn't made much headway with the textbooks. Mere days ago that fact would have irritated her no end. But today she didn't care. She really didn't. The university's art department had given her six weeks to make her recommendations. She doubted that a few lost nights would make any difference in the grand scheme of things. At the moment it was much more important for her to...

To what? Spend time with Jack? Go to parties? Kiss the man?

Then what? the voice of reason cautioned. Jack jumped from buildings for a living. Such work would necessitate his leaving Denver. Probably for long periods of time.

Eleanor frowned at the intrusive whisperings of her own conscience.

Drat it all, she wouldn't worry about what the future might bring. Not today. Not when she'd had such fun.

But as she readied herself for work the inner warning returned to her full force.

What was she thinking? the little voice railed. She'd spent the months putting her life back together, finding a job, an apartment, preparing herself emotionally for motherhood—and she knew she still had adjustments that needed to be made. She had no business becoming involved with a man who risked his well-being every time he went to work.

The very idea was enough to make her cringe. As far as she was concerned, life itself was risk enough. What possible reason could a man have for courting danger? Surely being a stuntman made a statement about Jack's character. Perhaps he had a death wish, as she had once accused.

The thought made her shudder. She wouldn't think about that now. She couldn't think about any of it.

Stuffing her arms through the sleeves of her coat, she grabbed her bag and her cane and made her way downstairs. Once at her landladies' door, she tapped softly, not wanting to wake the women if they were still sleeping, but hoping they were ready for visitors.

The door squeaked open. "Eleanor!" Minnie exclaimed. "Good morning. Would you like to join me for some tea? *The Price Is Right* will be starting soon."

"No, thank you, Minnie. I have to get to work. I just wondered if you still had the phone number of my reader."

"I penciled it onto a scrap of paper and hung it on my bulletin board. Did you want it, dear?"

"Yes. I need to cancel my session tonight."

Minnie made a clucking noise with her tongue. "You're not catching that flu bug that's roaming around, are you?"

"No, I just…I have to work," she lied, not wanting to admit to Minnie that cowardice was her only motivation for canceling the appointment. Her relationship with Jack was developing much too quickly. Perhaps if they had some time apart, she would be able to look at things far more objectively.

"What a shame. Your reader is such a nice young man."

"Yes, I…" Eleanor cocked her head when she heard the distant whine of a bus.

Minnie must have noted the sound, as well, because she patted Eleanor's arm. "You run along, dear. I'll make the call."

A rush of relief poured through Eleanor's system. "Really? You don't mind?"

"Not at all. You hurry so you don't miss your ride. I'd hate for you to have to work even longer to make up for a late arrival."

"Thanks, Minnie."

Unfolding her cane, Eleanor rushed onto the stoop and from there to the sidewalk. As she did so, she heard the squeal of brakes and the thump of the bus's door.

"Hey, Eleanor!" Burt called. "Need a lift to the bus stop?"

She laughed, recognizing the driver's voice. "Yes, I do."

"Then hop on."

Twenty minutes later she was once again in the cool confines of The Flick. As she tied the apron around her waist and reached for the tape recorder to determine her duties, she reassured herself that she was "safe." Jack wouldn't know how to find her. He wouldn't come for their reading session later that night. By the time she saw him, she would have sorted out the apprehension that had pummeled her all morning. Then she would plan the best way to handle the situation.

By the time she met Jack again, she would be completely prepared.

JACK SWORE when the cellular phone in his pocket bleeped just as he was sipping hot coffee from the cup he held. Setting it down on the bench, he swiped his wet hand down his pants and turned on the phone.

"Yeah."

"Is this Jack?"

He frowned, not recognizing the voice on the other end.

"This is Jack MacAllister."

"Oh, good. This is Minnie Vanderbilt. Eleanor Rappaport's landlady."

"Yes, Minnie." He leaned forward, wondering what she could possibly want from him at this time of day.

"Miss Rappaport meant to call you herself, but she had a bus to catch."

Jack waited for the rest of the message, but when none was forthcoming, he realized Minnie was waiting for some kind of response.

"I see," he murmured, wondering what he should say.

Evidently Minnie was satisfied with his response because she continued, "Eleanor has to work late today—a double shift, I suppose. She does that sometimes."

Another pause.

"Mmm," Jack grunted.

"Any-hoo, she won't be able to meet you tonight."

Jack frowned, staring across the street, his eyes narrowing. "I see."

"It's a shame, really. Oftentimes she just sits at that candy counter with nothing at all to do between shows. That makes for a long evening."

"I'm sure it does."

There was a pause and Jack wondered if his response hadn't been enough. Then Minnie said, "I don't suppose you could meet her there...at her work?"

Jack straightened, immediately pleased. "Wouldn't her employer object?"

Minnie made a soft snort. "Not at all. As long as the popcorn is fresh, the customers happy and the tickets distributed, Eleanor's boss is content. That's why so many college students work there. Barbara allows them to study during the showings."

"I'll certainly consider the idea, Minnie," Jack said, even though he didn't need to think about it at all. He suspected the real reason Eleanor had canceled the evening. He was getting too close, he was treading on her comfort zone—and she felt she needed some time to fortify her defenses.

This time she was dead wrong.

Punching End, he slid the cell phone back into his pocket.

He didn't intend to let Eleanor have the time to add one more brick to that emotional wall she'd built around herself. Not one single brick.

ELEANOR WAS BEGINNING to wish she'd never told Minnie that she needed to work late. Since birth Eleanor had never displayed a talent for lying— she'd always been caught. Either by her mother or by some resulting consequence that had punished her for her folly.

Today had proved to be no different. From the

moment she'd arrived at The Flick, the Fates had been more than happy to show her the error of her ways. Since eleven o'clock that morning, two employees had called in sick for the evening showings, and Eleanor's mythical double shift was swiftly becoming a reality.

Her hand bumped against the candy counter, and she swore under her breath as the unpopped kernels of corn bounced from the measuring cup she held and scattered across the floor.

"You really shouldn't say such words within earshot of the customers."

At the low, silken comment, she jumped, causing another wave of kernels to skitter onto the tile.

"Jack." His name left her lips in a whisper, and Eleanor stood rooted to the floor, sure that she'd imagined the voice. After all, she'd done nothing but think about the man since her arrival at the theater.

Not that her ruminations had solved anything. She was as undecided about how to proceed as she had been that morning. She simply couldn't seem to find a way to neatly classify the man, stuff him in an emotional cubbyhole and develop a plan of attack.

"You're looking pained. Did you burn yourself?"

It was evident from the amusement in his tone that he knew very well that she hadn't even touched the heating element inside the popping machine.

Deciding that a confrontation would be the best course of action, she whirled to face him more completely—nearly slipping when the soles of her shoes skidded over the kernels of corn as if they were greased ball bearings.

"What are you doing here?"

"We had an appointment."

"My landlady was going to call and cancel."

"She did call. Then she suggested I join you here. She thought you could use the diversion."

Diversion. Such an innocuous word could in no way describe this man.

Remembering the measuring cup in her hand, Eleanor used it to her advantage. Turning her attention to the popper, she bought herself some time by dumping the kernels in the bin and locking the mechanism in place.

"I'm afraid she misled you. I won't have time to work tonight. We've had two employees call in sick, so we're very shorthanded."

"Fine."

She waited, expecting to hear his footfalls moving away from the candy counter. Instead she gasped when he moved behind her, his body brushing hers as he passed in the wrong direction, one that would lead him to a dead end of candy and chocolate bars.

"You can't get out that way," she said needlessly, her voice oddly breathless after the brief rubbing of bodies.

"I don't want to get out. I'll stay and help."

"What?" she gasped in disbelief, just as Barbara ran down the steps from the projection room.

"Good. You're hired!" Babs called as she raced to the ticket booth.

Eleanor scowled and lowered her voice so that only Jack could hear. "You can't help."

"Your boss just said I could."

"She didn't know what she was agreeing to...what you were offering."

"I think she got the general idea."

Eleanor scrambled to think of another reason why he should leave.

"You don't know what you're doing, Jack, and I don't have time to explain how Babs likes things to be done. Any minute a bus from a nearby retirement home will arrive, and people will be lining up six deep."

"If I need help, I'll ask. In the meantime, I'll wing it."

"'Wing it'?" Eleanor's lips thinned in impatience. "Jack, really, I don't think—"

"Let him stay!" Barbara called as she huffed past again, this time making her way to the office. "We need someone to cover the till."

Eleanor clenched her teeth. She had no real comeback for such reasoning. Except for coins, she couldn't identify the money she received. She was accustomed to having someone else man the cash register.

But that didn't mean she had to surrender gracefully.

Eleanor waited until she was sure Barbara was out of earshot. As soon as the woman's desk drawers began to bang, she pointed a finger in Jack's direction. "Don't you dare make a mess of things tonight as some sort of retribution."

"Retribution?"

"For canceling our appointment."

"Why would I want retribution? After all, you couldn't help the fact that you had to work late."

Eleanor snapped her mouth shut before she could offer any more incriminating information on her own behalf. Too late she wished she'd had the sense to call Minnie and determine exactly what the woman had told Jack in her telephone conversation.

But such thoughts were useless now. She would have to make the best of the next few hours, keep Jack in his place and her thoughts on her job.

Easier said than done.

Moments later customers began arriving for an all-night Joan Crawford marathon, and she and Jack were too busy to converse. But that didn't mean she wasn't aware of him. Of his strong body leaning against hers, his hand touching her back, her arm, her shoulder. His voice calm and unflappable despite the rush to satisfy their customers before the movie started.

By the time the first strains of music came from the theater, Eleanor was exhausted—from the demands of her mind as well as the demands of the candy counter.

"Eleanor, you take a break," Barbara called as she stepped from the ticket booth. "I feel bad enough keeping you here for a double shift, the least I can do is order some takeout."

"That isn't necessary." Eleanor immediately rejected the offer, knowing it was extended to Jack as well. She wanted him gone, away from the close confines of the old theater and the floorboards that constantly squeaked to announce his presence. She might be willing to consider a relationship with him, but she was not ready to invite him into every facet of her life—especially her work.

Although she would never want to admit such a thing to Barbara or her mother, Eleanor found it galling that her current occupation was that of a hired hand at a candy counter. She'd once created things with her hands. She'd painted murals the size of three-story buildings. Now she couldn't tell the difference between a one-dollar bill and a twenty.

But if Barbara had sensed an iota of her hesitance, she gave no indication. "Hush, I insist. You've got to eat. Both of you."

So the matter was settled, even if Eleanor didn't agree with the outcome.

As soon as Eleanor could, she stepped out of the narrow walkway behind the glass case. She had to get some air, put some space between her and Jack.

"Where are you going?" Jack asked.

She stiffened, knowing she couldn't tell him the truth—*away from you*—so she settled for a muffled grunt and made her way to the narrow staircase. Taking a right at the landing, she moved into the space that had once been the old cry room. In days gone by, mothers with nursing babies or fretful children could bring their charges upstairs to a small glass-enclosed cubicle that faced the main screen. Speakers had been bolted to the wall to allow such visitors to hear the movie and the darkness allowed them a modicum of privacy.

Eleanor prayed that Jack would give her some time to herself, but she didn't really think he would.

Therefore she was not terribly surprised when his footsteps joined hers on the well-worn treads.

Sighing, she trailed her fingers along the wall until she reached the backs of the chairs, settling into one of the half dozen seats.

Jack's low whistle nearly escaped her as she propped her feet on the armrest of the chair in front of her and breathed in relief at finally being allowed to sit down. Her feet ached and her calf muscles were protesting the number of times she'd had to run downstairs for new supplies. She had less than four weeks before her due date, and she was feeling increasingly uncomfortable. But she wasn't about to take a leave of absence until she had to. She valued her last weeks of total independence before she settled into her duties as "mommy."

"This is quite the place."

She heard Jack move to the window overlooking the theater.

"Haven't you ever been here before?" she asked, closing her aching eyes and leaning her head back.

"I told you. I'm not from this area."

She shrugged. "I keep forgetting."

"How old is this building?"

"It was built in 1921 as a performance hall but was soon adapted into a movie theater."

In her mind she could picture every inch of the restored building. As a child she'd come here almost every Saturday—especially during the summer. She'd always been fascinated with the ornate Egyptian carvings that covered the walls and rimmed the ceiling.

Barbara had been careful to refurbish the building in its original style, using old photographs as a guide—and for that Eleanor was glad. She would have been disappointed if even one twinkling light had been omitted from overhead. All too well she remembered the way the ceiling had been painted to resemble a moonlit sky sparkling with distant stars—which weren't really stars, but were shimmering bulbs embedded in the plaster.

"Barbara must have spent a fortune restoring this place."

"Barbara calls it her labor of love. She and a group of history buffs raised nearly a half million dollars to rebuild The Flick. Over fifty craftsmen were hired to recreate the original plaster moldings. The seats and carpets were specially dyed and the modern film-projection equipment carefully hidden. She's already applied for listing on the National Register."

From the movie below, Joan Crawford was saying, "Kiss me. Kiss me now."

Eleanor shifted uncomfortably, gesturing in the general direction of the speaker on the wall. "There's a knob at the bottom if you want to adjust the volume."

Uneasily she noted that when Jack turned the sound down, he created an even more cozy silence between them. When she heard the squeak of the seat next to her and felt Jack's warmth easing into her skin, she stiffened.

"You're rather jumpy tonight," he commented.

"Not at all." But the insistence rang false, even to her own ears.

"Do you want to tell me why you canceled our study session?"

"Isn't it obvious?" she asked, waving her hand in a dismissive gesture, then wishing she hadn't when she came in contact with his arms.

"You can't use your job as an excuse. Barbara admitted that you volunteered for the extra shift this afternoon. You had Minnie call me this morning."

Damn.

"Have I done something to offend you? Maybe I shouldn't have stayed so long last night. Or is that the problem? Has our intimacy made you nervous?"

She gave a peal of laughter that she hoped sounded genuine.

"Of course not."

"Then why are you avoiding me?"

"I'm not avoiding you."

"Yes. You are."

She jerked when he touched her cheek.

"I thought you enjoyed yourself yesterday." His tone was low and silky.

"I had a wonderful time at the party."

"What about later? In your apartment. When I kissed you? Held you in the darkness?"

A tightness gathered in her throat, and she swallowed in an effort to clear it.

"I don't know what you mean. The party was fun. I told you that."

He touched her again, cradling her cheek in his

palm, his fingers curling around the back of her head.

"What about the way we were necking on the couch?"

Necking. There was such an intimacy to his choice of words.

"Did I make a mistake in thinking you enjoyed it as much as I did?"

How was she supposed to respond to his question without sounding like a fool or a weak-kneed spinster? They both knew that her ardor had not been feigned.

She felt him moving toward her, felt his breath sweep over her skin.

"Am I making a mistake now?"

Eleanor couldn't respond. Not when she wanted him to kiss her. The fact that she would curse herself for her weakness when her head grew clear again didn't matter. All that mattered was this moment.

This man.

This kiss.

Chapter Ten

Jack's lips took hers, so sweetly that it might have been their first encounter. Deftly, surely he explored the curves of her mouth, her cheek and her jaw.

Her fingers curled into the cotton of his shirt, drawing him closer, needing more of him than he was giving. Her lips eagerly parted, and when his tongue slipped inside, she reeled from the immediate pleasure that flooded her veins.

Never had she responded so fully to a man.

Never.

Eleanor jerked free, the word echoing in her brain.

What was she doing? This was a temporary employee, nothing more. He would leave her. He had to leave her. His life was a long series of temporary stays. She would not—*could not*—allow herself to grow emotionally needy.

Needy.

Dear Heaven above, she already needed him so much. Wanted him. Craved him.

"What's wrong?"

She jumped when he clasped her shoulders from

behind. Whirling, she held up her hands as if to ward him off.

"I think you'd better go."

"Why?"

"I—" Words failed her, so she summoned as much dignity as she could scrape together.

"What are you afraid will happen, Eleanor?"

"*Afraid?*" she sputtered.

He held her arms, preventing her from backing out of the aisle so that she could escape.

"Yes. I think you're afraid."

"Of what?" she demanded.

"Of me, of life, of your pregnancy. Yourself."

Eleanor was so shocked she would have struck him if her hands were free.

"How dare you!"

"I dare because it's time you heard the truth."

"And what makes you think your high-handed opinion is the truth?"

"Because I see the way you live. You closet yourself in this theater by day and your apartment by night. You've made no preparations for a baby that is due in a few weeks, and you patently ignore the fact that time is ticking way."

"I lead a very busy life."

"Do you? I haven't seen any evidence of such a claim."

"Do you think that if you take the blind woman to dinner, dance with her, kiss her, you'll brighten an otherwise dismal life? You must have a very high opinion of yourself."

"Dammit, that's not what I meant."

"Then what did you mean?" She balled her hands into fists and thrust them against his chest, forcing him to release her. Taking a step back, she demanded, "Who are you to judge me or my life? You know nothing about me. Nothing at all."

"So tell me."

"Tell you what? What sorts of gory details do you need? Do you want to know how I lost my sight? Do you want to hear about the way a pickup skidded across an icy road and slammed into the side of my car?"

A thick silence flowed around them like hot tar. But now that the floodgates had broken, Eleanor couldn't stop.

"The whole incident was a freak accident. I wasn't even supposed to be on that road. I was thinking about my upcoming exhibit, missed my exit and was forced to drive to the next one. The weather had been bad all day, so I was creeping along at a snail's speed. Then—bam! I hit that patch of black ice and slid down the hill, adding to a two-car pileup."

She offered a bitter laugh. "Even then I was fine—not a scratch. But like a fool I released my safety belt and was trying to get out when the pickup hit the same patch of ice."

A shivering tension spilled around her, augmented by the harsh, rapid breathing of her companion. Sensing she had his attention, she continued.

"I had so many plans, so many dreams. I was going to have an exhibit at the National Gallery. I wanted to see the Eiffel Tower. I wanted to take skydiving lessons and meet Robert Redford and make love under the aurora borealis.''

Her words echoed in the tiny room, and her energy drained away as quickly as it had come.

''Is it any wonder that I take things slowly? That I plan more carefully? I'm rebuilding myself from the inside out—and I have absolutely no idea what the future will bring. But I've survived.''

Her anger left her in one whooshing exhalation.

''I've survived.'' She took a deep shuddering breath. ''And don't you preach to me about whether or not I've made proper preparations for this baby. This is my baby. Mine. It will be no one's responsibility but mine.''

''A fact that has you scared to death.''

She inhaled sharply, then curled her hands into fists to keep from reaching toward the sound of that voice and slapping him.

''I think you'd better go.''

He grasped her arms. ''Why? Because it's safer? Easier? Haven't you been taking the easy road for far too long? You've made a nice little life for yourself, but it isn't a bit challenging nor is it satisfying. You've abandoned your art and delayed putting yourself on the transplant list—even though the surgery to your eyes could have been performed safely despite your pregnancy.

She wrenched out of his grip. ''You've been talking to my landladies again.''

''Hell, yes. I won't get any of this information from you. You shy away from any sort of personal conversation. You won't let me into your life—''

"And why should I?"

The little room echoed with her sharp retort. Eleanor took a moment to calm herself, then continued. "I don't know you well enough to confide anything in you. You're a man I met little more than a week ago, yet you seem to have formed some very strong opinions about my life. But it's *my* life. You won't be here a year from now, or two, or three. Will you?"

The silence was underscored by the muffled sound of the distant movie.

"No," he finally admitted. "I suppose not."

Although she had been expecting the words, she was not prepared for the keen disappointment they brought.

"I think you'd better go," she whispered.

"Eleanor, I—"

Suddenly weary, she silenced him with a wave of her hand. "Go. Please."

She sensed his reluctance but finally heard his footfalls disappearing from the room and down the hall. Only then did she sink into one of the seats, her arms wrapping around her middle.

"We don't need him, do we, little one?"

So why did she suddenly feel so bereft?

I'VE SURVIVED.

The words echoed in Jack's head long after he left The Flick and made his way to his temporary apartment.

Little did Eleanor know, but she'd echoed his own thoughts of late. For some time he'd grown increasingly restless with his life-style. Not so much his work—there were still exciting moments and challenging situations. No, his dissatisfaction came more from the time away from work. Empty hours.

So what did he want that he didn't have? Someone like Eleanor to meet him at the door?

He had to admit that he looked forward to their skirmishes. He counted the hours until they could be together again.

But was that what he wanted? A more tangible relationship? A *lasting* relationship? With Eleanor?

No. He didn't know this woman. He had no room in his life for ties. He was a free spirit, a man known for his solitary status. And let's face it, he didn't have a job that many women would put up with.

But that reputation hadn't made him nearly as happy as the past few days had done.

Sighing, Jack unlocked the Corvette and slid behind the wheel. But he didn't immediately start the engine. Tapping his fingers on the wheel, he pondered all he'd discovered about Eleanor that day. She was such a vibrant woman. If only she wouldn't dampen her passions. If only she didn't need anger to set her will free.

Passion.

That's what Eleanor had brought to his life. Passion. And it had been so long since he'd felt the emotion himself.

Dammit. When she'd railed at him about all she'd once wanted to do, he'd wanted to shake her until she admitted that such dreams didn't have to die. They only had to be adapted to her new life.

If he could only make her admit such a thing herself.

But how?

WHEN JACK ARRIVED at Eleanor's apartment the following evening, it was obvious that she was not in a playful mood. She'd donned a dull-colored shapeless jumper that reminded him of Jackie Kennedy, and her hair had been twisted into a knot at her nape. Her entire bearing radiated the message No Trespassing as clearly as if she'd hung a sign around her neck.

"I think it's time we got some work done on the books."

He grinned openly at her militant expression but kept his voice matter-of-fact.

"Fine."

It was clear that she'd expected some sort of argument. Rather than giving her one, he unzipped his jacket, threw it over the back of the couch, then sat down.

"Which one do you want me to read first?"

"We may as well start with the Forbes and Dunne."

She sat on the chair opposite, folding her hands over her stomach as primly as a spinster.

Again he grinned. Opening the book, he asked, "Do you want me to start with the preface or the first chapter?"

"Preface."

He began reading, knowing that she expected him to make some sort of sensual game of the words—

and because she expected such a thing, he did just the opposite. His tone was carefully modulated, bland but not boring. He read slowly enough for her to evaluate the information, but not so slowly as to irritate.

Through it all he found himself watching her, gauging her reaction, wondering if she knew how expressive her features could be. It was quite clear to him she wasn't concentrating on the literature— just as it was obvious that she was waiting for him to make some sort of sensual advance.

If she only knew how much he wanted to do just that. It took every ounce of control he possessed not to toss the book onto the couch, reach for her and pull her into his arms.

But he didn't do that. Since her outburst at the theater he'd begun to realize just how fragile her control was and just how much she hated the fact.

After finishing the closing arguments of the preface, Jack waited for some sort of comment from Eleanor.

None came.

Instead, she was looking at him as if she could see through the darkness to his very soul.

"You have a beautiful voice," she finally said.

The silence had stretched so taut between them that Jack had been about to accuse her of not paying attention.

"After all the work you've done with films, did you ever consider acting?" she continued.

"No."

"Why not?"

"I don't have patience for confinement."

"Confinement?"

"The endless waiting involved in preparing for a shot."

"But surely you must encounter much the same thing in your own line of work."

"Yes, but most of the time *I'm* the one doing the preparing. Besides which, acting can be pretty damned dull."

"As opposed to jumping off buildings?"

"Exactly."

Her brow furrowed slightly. "What is it about the stunt work that attracts you?"

"My job is different every day."

"Surely there's more to your reasons than that."

He was beginning to understand where her questions were leading. "You mean the element of risk."

"Many people might think you have a death wish."

"Many people? Or you?"

She shifted, obviously uncomfortable with the way he'd personalized her remark.

"You think I'm stupid to take such risks."

She vehemently shook her head. "Not stupid…careless."

"Why?" He leaned forward, resting his forearms on his knees and clasping his hands to keep from reaching out and dragging her closer. She looked so earnest, so self-righteous, so…

So damned appealing.

"I don't know why you would want to injure yourself."

"I take a great deal of time to ensure such a thing doesn't happen."

"But you can't plan for every contingency."

"No."

"So you've been hurt more than once on the job?"

"Yes."

"Seriously?"

He thought of the concussion he'd suffered during his last film. The reoccurring dreams that had ensued. Dreams that had brought him here. To this woman. To this moment.

"You haven't answered my question."

Jack sighed, knowing that he couldn't lie, but knowing the truth would merely validate her fears.

"Well?" she prompted.

"I've broken a bone or two."

"So why would you purposely court such dangers again?"

He racked his brain for some way to explain. But no matter how hard he thought, he couldn't find the words. Finally he said, "It's what I do. It's who I am."

Rather than reassuring her, his response seemed to have the opposite effect. Her skin grew pale.

"That's what I thought," she murmured. Then, waving in his direction, she ordered, "Go on with your reading."

But it was not so easy for him to continue. Not when her brow had creased in a frown and her fingers plucked nervously at the fabric on the arm of her chair.

Finally he sighed and put the book away.

After several minutes of silence she noticed that he had stopped reading, and her lips twisted in a rueful grimace.

"It seems we aren't getting much work done tonight, either."

He waited a moment, then said, "You appear worried."

She opened her mouth as if to speak, then obviously stopped to choose her words carefully.

"In the past few days I've been giving our relationship a great deal of thought."

Relationship. The word sounded so much more complicated once it was spoken aloud.

"What have you decided?" he asked, wondering if this was the moment that she would tell him to leave. He'd been expecting her to terminate his services ever since their argument at The Flick.

"I'm not sure," she admitted, and he was surprised by her honesty. "I like you, Jack. I have enjoyed our time much more than I would have thought possible."

"But..." he prompted.

"But I don't know where we're headed."

He sighed, leaning forward and planting his elbows on his knees. Eleanor looked so earnest and vulnerable that he wanted to sweep her into his arms and banish her fears. But how could he reassure her when he didn't know how to proceed himself?

"I care for you, Eleanor." The words came

slowly from his mouth. Not because he regretted them, but because he had never offered them to another woman.

"What do you want from me? Sex? A good time? I'll warn you now that I'm too close to term to make love."

Her bluntness was completely out of character, and he sensed she was trying to shock him.

"Is that all you think I'm after?"

"I won't know until you tell me."

He exhaled sharply and stood, crossing to the window. Staring down at the quiet street, knowing that he had no easy answers to give.

"I'm not a man accustomed to emotional entanglements," he finally admitted.

"What a surprise." Her tone was mocking.

He smiled ruefully. "It has been a long time since I've attempted to woo a woman, so I suppose I'm not very good at it."

"Is that what you're trying to do? Woo me?"

"I don't know." He turned to her then, discovering that she had stood and closed the distance between them while he had been gazing out the window.

"Then what *do* you know?"

Her skin was so soft, so pale, so rich in the half-light. Looking at her, he was struck again by how beautiful she was.

"I don't want a professional relationship to the exclusion of all else."

The words melted out of his mouth before he had a chance to think about how much of himself he was revealing. But once they were said, he discovered that he didn't want to take them back. For a split second he felt the same rush of adrenaline, the same sense of danger he experienced in performing his stunts. He had bared himself to her emotionally, and now it was her turn to decide what would happen.

She stood so still, he might have thought she was looking right at him, but when she reached for him, her aim was short, and he stepped forward so that the connection could be made.

"I've had a lot of changes in my life this past year," she said, touching his shoulder, then curving her fingers around his nape. "I may need some time to become accustomed to sharing my evenings with another person."

Jack felt as if he were walking on the edge of a precipice. "I don't think your request is out of line."

"I would also like to feel that I could place a few demands on you."

"Of course."

She took a deep breath, and he felt the tension in her body subside.

"Then I suppose we have an agreement. Our relationship is no longer one of blind lady and reader."

He chuckled, unable to resist sliding his arms around her waist and drawing her close.

"Nope. Now it's just you and me. A woman and a man."

Then he was kissing her, knowing that nothing could ever be the same between them. He was no longer an innocent party in this bargain. He had willingly committed himself to her, even though he hadn't told her so many things she needed to know—his reason for being here...

And the way they'd first met on a windswept hill near Estes Park.

Chapter Eleven

"Hello, Barbara."

"Jack."

Eleanor stiffened when she heard the voices on the other side of the storeroom door. She and Jack had been seeing each other for more than two weeks, but the sound of his voice still never failed to thrill her.

"Is Eleanor in?"

"She's just about to finish her shift."

"Good. I've got plans for her this afternoon."

"Really? Care to share them?"

"Not yet. Eleanor has ears like a bat, you know, and quite a penchant for eavesdropping."

Eleanor dropped the broom she'd been using, then swore. Somehow that blasted man had caught her in the act.

Barbara merely laughed. "Have fun, you two."

Her footsteps disappeared down the corridor, and within moments, the storeroom door creaked open.

"Are you ready to go?"

She stiffened at his breezy tone.

"I thought I told you that I didn't want to work on the textbooks tonight."

"You did."

"So where are we going?"

"Lamaze."

Her mouth dropped in astonishment. "What?"

"You heard me. According to Minnie and Maude—"

"Will you stop talking to them!"

"—it's past time you were taking your classes."

"I'm not going to Lamaze classes with you."

A gust of warm air blew past her as he opened the door and ushered her outside.

"Why not?"

"Because it's so...so..."

"Personal?" He leaned close to whisper in her ear. "I want to get personal with you, Eleanor. Very personal. And that includes helping you to prepare for this baby."

"But..."

"Three weeks. We only have three weeks to get ready."

"I..."

"There's furniture to buy, a room to prepare, little things to pick out."

She stopped in her tracks, causing him to bump into her side when he didn't anticipate her sudden stubbornness.

"Why are you doing this?"

She felt his fingers touch her cheek, her throat, then dip to spread wide over her abdomen. As if in response, the baby—who was always more active when Jack was around—kicked his hand.

"Because there's a life in here." His tone held such awe that she shivered in something akin to delight. "It's time we made it welcome, don't you think?"

"Jack, I—"

When she couldn't continue, he drew her close, tucking her head beneath his chin. And in that instant she didn't care that the two of them were embracing in a very public place.

"Eleanor, I know you're scared."

Her fingers clutched handfuls of his shirt.

"You planned to have this baby when you had your sight, your career and your well-ordered life. Then things changed—drastically, suddenly. And you're afraid of what the future will bring—not just for you, but for your child."

A lump the size of a baseball seemed to wedge in her throat, and tears stung the backs of her eyes. How was it possible that this man, this stranger, saw into her soul so completely?

"I love my baby," she whispered.

"I know you do."

"But there's a part of me that is afraid that if I really think about it and our future together, I'll…jinx things. Despite all the tests that have been made since the accident, a part of me is still afraid something might…go wrong."

"I know, sweetheart." He drew her closer, lifting her on tiptoe and supporting her weight.

"But nothing is going to happen, you'll see. This

baby is going to be happy and healthy and eager to see his mama, and you haven't left yourself much time to get things in order for his arrival.''

"*Her* arrival,'' she insisted, half laughing, half sobbing.

"You mean you don't know the sex of the baby yet? Minnie told me you had an ultrasound.''

"I had the doctor keep the results secret.''

"Do you have a tape of the test?''

"Yes.''

"Good. Then as soon as we get back from Lamaze, I'll take a gander at the little squirt and let you know whether we'll be painting the nursery blue or pink.''

"Yellow. I hate stereotypes.''

Offering her one last hug, he led her toward the car. "Whatever. Just don't take the gender-equity nonsense too far and make him play with dolls.''

Laughing, Eleanor slid into the car seat, feeling somehow lighter and freer than she had in months, as if by finally sharing her fears she had liberated herself from monsters she hadn't even known she possessed.

"Jack?'' she said as he slid into his own seat.

"Yes.''

She reached for his hand and twined their fingers together.

"Thanks.''

He kissed the backs of her knuckles. "Save your thanks, sweetheart. You ain't seen nothing yet.''

IN THE END the small room next to Eleanor's bedroom was painted with soft, mint-green hills and a pale-blue sky. Unbeknownst to her, Jack enlisted the aid of the art department at the university, and they gladly volunteered to paint the murals on the walls and intersperse them with wood cutouts of a picket fence, a little barn, tractors and animals.

Eleanor was so touched by the way Jack made the nursery stimulating for the baby, yet three-dimensionally artistic for herself. Until she ''toured'' the room with her hands, she hadn't realized that this was the very reason she'd avoided decorating a nursery for so long. She'd wanted things perfect, but had found the limitations of her blindness getting in the way.

Not to be outdone, it was Eleanor who chose woolly scatter rugs, flannel receiving blankets, soft cotton linens and gauzy voile draperies. She accessorized the room with stuffed animals and toys with barnyard scenes, trusting Jack's assertion that the ultrasound he'd seen was definitely that of a boy— even though Minnie was convinced it would be a girl. Somehow, Eleanor knew that Jack would be right. Just as he'd been right about so many things before.

At times it amazed her how completely her life had changed since Jack had come along. He'd given her a new perspective on life and its challenges. And while she still wasn't completely resigned to her blindness, he'd infused her with a courage to try everything she could to put her life on track. At the urging of her doctor, she'd put her name on the corneal transplant list. Now it was a matter of waiting for a donor and the operation. After that...well, no matter what happened to her sight after the surgery, she was determined to find a way back into the art world she'd loved so much.

"HEY, RUSSO. What's up?"

Victor stared at him over the top of his script. If Jack wasn't mistaken, Victor hadn't moved from the pile of papers and notebooks he'd spread over the coffee table, the couch and the floor. His eyes were red rimmed from exhaustion.

"Not much."

"You look busy."

Victor grimaced. "The producer for my latest project just informed me that the filming schedule has been moved up a month."

Jack offered him a sympathetic grimace. "That's too bad."

"Don't get too sad about it. There's a message for you on the machine. Palermo needs you back to reshoot some scenes. One-Eye is already in his room packing. He's made arrangements to fly home to-night."

"It stinks, Jack," One-Eye called from the bed-room. "I just bought another week's worth of Rock-ies tickets—right over the dugout!"

Jack's mood immediately darkened. Swearing un-der his breath he crossed to the answering machine and punched the button. When the director insisted Jack return his call, and explained the reasons be-hind the emergency, Jack's anger deepened—not so much because of the need for refilming. This wouldn't be the first time Jack and his crew had been summoned back for new footage.

No, it was Eleanor. He didn't want to leave her just yet. Not when the baby was due in the next ten days.

So what was he going to do?

Jack went to the bedroom and leaned against the doorjamb. "If you have Rockies tickets, why don't you stay for another few days?"

One-Eye shot him a knowing look. "Because one of us has to get back to L.A. right away, and I figured you'd want to spend more time with your gal."

When Jack didn't respond, One-Eye straightened from his packing. "What's up with you?" he asked, his gaze intent. "I would have thought you'd be pleased with my decision."

"I am."

One-Eye snorted. "So why do you look as if someone shot your dog?"

Was he really that transparent?

Jack studied One-Eye consideringly, wondering how much information he should give the man.

One-Eye held up both hands as if he could ward off the scrutiny. "Hey, you don't have to tell me what's bugging you. But I bet I can guess."

"You think so, huh?"

One-Eye nodded, moving to the dresser and taking a swallow of the beer he'd left there. "I bet your current mood is due to that lady friend you've been romancing."

"Maybe."

One-Eye snorted. "You know I'm right. You just

don't want to admit it.'' He grinned. ''Frankly, I think she's perfect for you.''

''Why?''

''Because she can't see how ugly you really are.'' One-Eye chuckled at his own joke, set his beer on the dresser and began rolling his socks into neat balls. ''So tell Papa One-Eye what's wrong.''

''Nothing is wrong.''

''And I'm the pope.''

Jack sighed, wishing he'd never allowed this conversation to continue.

''If you ask my opinion,'' One-Eye went on, undaunted, ''the woman's a knockout.''

Jack couldn't account for the instant irritation the comment brought. Nor could he account for the surge of protectiveness he felt, the primitive sense of ownership.

''But I'd be careful if I were you,'' One-Eye continued.

''Why?'' Jack queried.

One-Eye eyed him for some time before finally saying, ''In our business we can't afford distractions, and we certainly can't afford to go soft. This woman's what we used to call a 'keeper' in my day and age. She's the sort that brings to mind wedding bells and picket fences.''

''And that's a bad thing?''

''In our line of work? Hell, yes! It's like I was saying—a girl like that will worry that you'll get hurt. She might even start telling you what kinds of jobs you should take—or insist you quit.'' He grew sober. ''Make very sure of what you want as an end result for this relationship. You're a born stuntman, and that's the way it ought to be. You could never be happy if a woman insisted you give up the work.'' One-Eye moved to a pile of shirts.

Jack found his attention wandering—especially now that One-Eye had said aloud the things that Jack had kept to himself for so long.

Eleanor was a woman who deserved commitment—needed commitment. But was he such a man? Moreover, was he a man worthy of becoming an instant father?

He'd never given the idea much thought in the past. His life-style didn't lend itself to entanglements, and he'd always shied away from them in the past. Just as One-Eye had said, a stuntman had to be willing to take risks in order to get the best effects. Safety was tantamount, but there was still a shred of the daredevil in every job he did.

Jack already knew that Eleanor didn't approve of his job. She thought he had some sort of death wish—or at the very least that he was careless with his health. If they were to build a more permanent relationship...

Whoa. What was he thinking? Eleanor Rappaport was a great person. Beautiful, talented, vulnerable and sexy. But he didn't really want to tie himself to her permanently.

Did he?

He took a deep breath, the thought reverberating in his head. With it came the memories of the time they'd spent together, the passion she'd inspired, the zest for life.

These past few weeks he'd been happier than he'd been in a long time, Jack realized. He enjoyed Eleanor's company—no, he craved it. He couldn't imagine saying goodbye. He didn't want to say goodbye.

Not now.

Not ever.

Jack's innate energy returned with a rush. Turning, he strode out of the apartment. There wasn't any time to lose. He was going to have to leave Denver by the end of the week.

By then he wanted some sort of understanding.

ELEANOR KNEW she would remember the past few weeks for the rest of her life. She couldn't think of a time when she had felt more alive, more in tune with every nuance of life surrounding her. Time and time again she found herself ruminating about Jack and the baby and the twists and turns that had brought them all together. Then she would laugh in triumph and joy.

Just this afternoon she'd been immersed in another of Jack's adventures. Earlier that day, he'd "kidnapped" her from The Flick and driven her into the cool foothills for a picnic. He'd provided a soft woolen throw, chilled lemonade, hearty sandwiches and filling salads. She'd eaten well, then curled up next to Jack while he'd described the shapes of the clouds overhead. She hadn't even been embarrassed when she'd nodded off to sleep, then awakened hours later to find herself tucked into her own bed, the heavenly scent of a rose beckoning to her from the pillow beside her.

What magic. What pure and utter magic. And all because Jack had stormed into her life and opened up a world of possibilities.

Eleanor chuckled secretly to herself.

"What's so funny about Postimpressionism?"

Jack's query brought her back to earth with a start, but she refused to let him know she hadn't been paying attention to his reading.

"I've always been immensely amused by Post-impressionism," she replied smugly. "You should see my reaction to Dadaism."

Jack snorted in disbelief, and she heard the book slam shut. The couch springs squeaked as he stood. "Have you got anything to eat?"

Over the past few nights she'd grown accustomed to such questions. The two of them had done their best to finish the evaluation of the university's textbooks—a feat that was nearly completed. In the process Eleanor had discovered that Jack's body burned energy at such a high rate he was invariably hungry two hours after they'd dined. Ruefully she wished she could say the same about her own body—especially lately. Nevertheless, she found herself catering to his whims, stocking her refrigerator with sandwich meats, pickles and vegetables.

"I got some of that smoked ham you like," she said, leaning her head against the back of the couch. That was another change that had occurred. She no longer sat in the chair, but curled up next to him, absorbing the vibration of his voice as it rumbled in his chest.

"Do you want something?"

"No." She thought of the Chinese food they'd had for dinner. She still felt stuffed to the gills. And with swollen feet and a stomach the size of the Goodyear blimp, she didn't feel much like tempting fate.

"What about a drink?"

"That would be great."

He returned a few minutes later, bringing with him the scents of fresh bread, ham and jalapeño peppers.

Her nose wrinkled. "Those peppers you left in my refrigerator are going to eat a hole in your stomach."

"Nah. If that were true, they would have done so long ago."

He settled on the couch and she heard the clank of his plate as he put it on the coffee table in front of them.

"Here's your soda."

She took the cool can, popped the lid and sipped.

"So what are you going to recommend to the art department?" Jack inquired.

"I like the Wilkenson-Fosse version the best, don't you?"

She felt him shrug. "I'm the last person to give an opinion, but as a lay person, it was the easiest for me to assimilate."

"Good. I'll include your comment on the evaluation sheet."

He settled against her, but when he didn't eat, she knew there was more that he meant to say.

"So the job's finished?"

There was wariness to his tone.

"Yes. I guess it is." She couldn't prevent the heaviness that lodged in the pit of her stomach.

"We didn't make too bad a team."

Team. Yes, they'd been a wonderful team. Jack hadn't merely read to her. At her request, he'd offered his own feedback, he'd described pictures and illustrations and had even taken the time to record a few of the chapters on tape so that she could work on them while she was at The Flick.

"So, Eleanor," he said slowly. "What do we do now?"

She knew what he was asking. The original reason for their interaction had just been fulfilled. Jack no longer had a business excuse to come to this place. What remained were purely personal reasons.

"I guess you'll just have to content yourself with being my..."

Eleanor stopped. Her what? Her friend? Her companion? *Her lover?*

"Your boyfriend?" Jack supplied.

She wrinkled her nose. "That sounds very archaic."

"But the meaning hasn't changed. It still implies companionship, fondness. Intimacy."

She felt a nervous tension gripping her throat and thought of the fragrant rose on her pillow.

"So what do you say, Eleanor? D'you want to get intimate?"

His voice became a husky growl, adopting a Groucho Marx kind of humor—one that defused the inherent danger of the situation. So much so that she was able to douse her usual reserve and answer in a similarly lighthearted tone.

"Yes, I suppose I do."

"How intimate?"

She shivered, knowing that if she weren't so close to term, such a question would probably have led to an invitation to make love.

"I—I—" But she didn't know how to respond without sounding as desperate as she felt.

Fortunately, Jack didn't seem to need a reply, his hands swept over her back, awakening even more of her body to the headiness of his touch. Then his head dipped and his lips took hers.

In an instant, she was inundated with a wave of need. She couldn't ever remember her body feeling so alive, so hungry, so wanton.

Straining against Jack, she broke away to kiss his jaw, his neck, and the hollow between his collarbones while her fingers grappled with the buttons of his shirt. In no time at all, his skin was bared to her questioning fingers.

Jack shuddered, his body thrumming with a passion unlike any he'd ever known before. Never, in all his wildest imaginings had he thought that his senses could be so alive to any one woman. As Eleanor stroked his skin and nibbled at the corners of his lips, he fought for control even as a part of him was ready to throw caution to the wind and make love to her. Here and now.

But even as his arm snapped around her waist to haul her closer, a faint pressure nudged his stomach. Once. Twice. Frowning, he suddenly realized the source of the sensation.

The baby.

The baby that Eleanor still secretly feared might have been harmed in the accident that occurred so long ago.

The thought was like being doused in cold water.

The baby. Eleanor had already told him she was too close to term to make love and he shied away from anything that might cause Eleanor any more worry or pain.

Especially after everything he'd already done— the accident...masquerading as a stranger...

Eleanor whimpered in frustration as he kissed her eyes, her cheeks, her lips, then held her to him, refusing to take things any further.

"Soon," he whispered.

His promise wasn't just to her, but to himself. The time had long since come to offer Eleanor a true confession of his reasons for being in Denver and his effect on her life.

Eleanor snuggled against him, placing a kiss on his bare chest and he shuddered with barely suppressed passion.

But not tonight.

Let him have one more evening of this—warmth, affection, sweet anticipation. Then, tomorrow he would make the hardest admission of his life.

He could only hope she would forgive him for everything.

Chapter Twelve

Jack rehearsed what he would say to Eleanor time and time again, never really finding a satisfactory way to disclose where they'd first met. When Palermo informed him that the shooting schedule would only involve four weekdays, Jack procrastinated in telling her again. He kept thinking that if he waited a little longer, until their relationship had eased from its businesslike origins to a purely personal one, he would be able to make her understand why he'd kept their first meeting a secret.

For the most part his plan seemed to work. Each hour they spent with each other intensified the passion they felt, as well as the tenderness.

When he told her he would be out of town for a few days, he was pleased at her obvious disappointment. It made returning to Denver that much easier.

They spent the night before his departure in Eleanor's apartment. She'd prepared dinner for them both, then they'd sat cuddled in front of the television while he gave a play-by-play of a movie that featured some of his own stunts. But when he saw her eyelids begin to droop, he knew it was time to go.

She stood when he did, still holding his hand.

"I'd better go."

"Why?"

He touched the tip of her nose. "Because you're falling asleep."

She grimaced. "Sorry."

"Don't be. You're awfully cute when you're sleepy."

They were making their way to the door, one step at a time. But as they passed another archway, which Jack had always assumed was a closet, he noted a narrow staircase.

"What's up there?" he asked, pausing.

"The apartment has two levels. Since I only use this floor, I keep the door closed."

"Show me."

"Why?" One of her brows lifted. "Are you thinking of moving in?"

The words hung in the air, filling the room with an indescribable sexual tension. He knew that she'd uttered the comment as a quip, but now that it had been said, its meaning was altogether more serious.

"I don't know, are you asking?"

He thought she would respond with an immediate refusal. Instead, she ignored the question completely and said, "Come upstairs and I'll show you."

She led up the worn treads to what had probably been intended as the servants' quarters when the home was built and still used as a one-family house. But upon reaching the landing, Jack realized that a great deal of work had been done to make the space habitable. Walls had probably been torn down, since the entire story was open. Gabled windows allowed moonlight to stream across the hardwood floors, and brass fixtures gleamed from a recent polishing.

"This is great," Jack said as Eleanor stopped in the center of the room beneath the highest portion of the sloping eaves. Above them a fan light waited to create a breeze.

"There's a switch somewhere that controls the power."

Jack released her hand to flip the lever and flood the room with a golden glow. Overhead the fan began to turn, causing a wafting breeze to stir the air.

"This is great," he said, turning slowly to survey every angle. A glimmer of an idea was beginning to surface in his brain, inspired by his surroundings. "Why don't you use it?"

She shrugged. "It seemed a waste of energy to bring furniture up here when there's space enough downstairs."

"So you don't have any plans for occupying it?"

She grew quite still, and he knew she was remembering her earlier suggestion that he might wish to move in.

"No. I don't have any plans."

He wondered if she knew how vulnerable she looked at that moment. It was clear that she was tempted to let him stay, but that she was just as tempted to renege on her offer.

"Do you want to use it?" she asked after some

time. "I…I mean, I know that going to school can be expensive and—"

"I'm not going to school."

"What?"

"I'm not enrolled in the university."

"But how—"

"I discovered you needed a volunteer, so I…volunteered."

It was obvious that she was still confused by the arrangement.

"But how did you discover I needed a reader?"

"I don't think it's important how—"

"Yes. It's incredibly important." Her expression grew fierce. "How did you know?"

He gave the least suspicious answer he could summon. "I was told by a mutual friend."

"My mother?"

"No."

"My father?"

"No."

"Then who?"

"Minnie."

Her mouth gaped. "Minnie?" she exclaimed.

"Yes."

"And how long have you known the woman?"

"Not long," he hedged.

"So when did she tell you I needed a reader?"

"Just after the university called with the arrangements. When Minnie told me you needed someone with an artistic background, I spoke to the volunteer center, and explained I had better qualifications than the student they'd enlisted."

"Don't you think you should have checked with me first?"

"I knew you'd say 'no.'"

"You're damn right, I would," she said, her hands balling into fists. "So why did you do it?"

"Because I wanted to meet you."

"That's preposterous."

"Is it?"

When she would have stormed past him to make her way down the stairs, he grabbed her shoulders. "Why? Because you're blind?"

"No. Because I'm no raving beauty. Other than Roger, I've never inspired anyone to take a second look."

"Then you must have spent your time with fools."

It became imperative to him that she understand his feelings.

"Eleanor, I think you are one of the most beautiful women I've ever met," he said slowly. If she'd known him better, she would have realized that he wasn't the kind of person to give compliments lightly. He'd never been prone to flowery speeches. He was a man of action, not words.

She made a dismissing snort. "Do you really expect me to believe you? As a stuntman, I'm sure you've seen—"

"Women with a great deal of expertise in arranging their hair, makeup, and wardrobe. That's not real beauty. Real beauty comes from within. From the soul."

He shifted, growing uncomfortable with his own

words. If there were only a way to break through her defenses.

"I arranged to work with you because you intrigued me. I thought you were pretty and smart, and I wanted the chance to meet you. But after a few minutes, all that was old news. I found that I wasn't content with a simple introduction. I wanted to know everything about you. I wanted to touch you. Kiss you." He drew her irretrievably closer. "Now, even that isn't enough."

She remained rigid in his embrace, so he kept quiet and still, allowing her the time to absorb his words. When she sagged against him, he experienced a relief like none he'd ever known.

"You believe me?"

She nodded.

"So will you let me use the room?"

Again she hesitated, and he tipped her head up so that the light would reveal every nuance of her expression. "I've been staying with Victor up to this point, but he's got his own out-of-town duties to fulfill."

"Oh."

He saw her features brighten ever so slightly, but she didn't speak.

"I promise, the arrangement will be purely platonic—at least until the baby arrives."

The blush that tinged her cheeks delighted him.

"I'll have a couch delivered and sleep up here whenever I come. That way, I can help you with the baby. I know your mother plans to help. And Minnie and Maude and the part time nanny they've hired.

But you might want a break during the middle of the night when no one else is around. No ties, no hassles. Just a simple, convenient arrangement so I can spend most of my time with you. I'll even put a deadbolt at the bottom of the stairs.''

"On your side, or on mine," she quipped. But then she squeezed his hand…

And he knew he could stay.

JACK SPENT four days in L.A., but the moment he returned to Denver, he had his plans completely formulated.

His first stop was the university's Art Department. Explaining his needs, he was soon given the help of a very earnest-looking young man whom the Dean had insisted was their best sculptor.

Taking the kid with him, Jack next went to an art supply house, where he insisted that the student order everything that a sculptor would need in his studio. When the purchases were complete, he thanked the artist, offered him a fifty-dollar bill for his services, then arranged for delivery of the equipment to Eleanor's home.

In order to prevent her from discovering his actions, he then called Eleanor, told her he'd arrived, and arranged to have her help him pick out a couch for his needs.

"Perhaps you should consider a bed," she suggested over the phone. "It wouldn't take up any more room."

He grinned, his body filling with a honeyed heat

at the mere sound of her voice. He'd missed her more than he would have thought possible.

"I don't think so," he drawled. "That would be much too tempting."

Then, after telling her when he would pick her up, he called Minnie Vanderbilt.

"Minnie, there's a delivery coming to Eleanor's apartment this afternoon. Will you let them in?"

"Why, yes!" she exclaimed eagerly. "What has she bought?"

"Nothing. I'm the one doing the buying."

"Oh?"

"It's a gift."

"What sort of gift?"

"Art supplies. I think it's time Eleanor went back to work."

"CLOSE YOUR eyes," Jack commanded. "While we've been gone, I've had a surprise delivered upstairs."

Eleanor snorted in disbelief. "Don't you think you're carrying things a little too far considering I can't see anything with my eyes opened or closed?"

"No. I don't. Close your eyes."

Taking her hand, he led her up the narrow staircase to the room above.

"I don't know why you think a new couch deserves all these theatrics. After all, I was there a few hours ago when you purchased the thing."

"Just keep your eyes closed and your mind open."

She frowned at that remark. "Why do I have to keep my mind open?" she asked suspiciously.

They reached the top of the stairs and he took her by the shoulders, urging her toward the huge worktable that had been assembled in the middle of the room.

"Because the couch isn't the only thing up here," he said softly, spying the plump leather sofa situated in the corner. The furniture store had kept their bargain to have it delivered immediately.

But that was the least of his worries at the moment. Right now, he had to make Eleanor understand what other pieces of furniture had been stored in the garret.

He took her hands and placed them on the flat, wooden surface.

Eleanor's lashes sprang open. "What is this?" But then her questing fingers found the lump of unformed clay and she frowned, recoiling as if she'd encountered a snake.

"I told you I was a painter, not a sculptor," she said, guessing immediately what he'd done.

"You can be anything you want to be."

Her chin lifted militantly. "So what makes you think I want to change what I am now?"

"Come on, Eleanor. You're working a dead-end job at a candy counter."

"I happen to like my work."

"You like your fellow workers, not the actual job."

She pursed her lips together.

"What you do is great for what it is. The job pays

the bills and gives you flexible hours. Beyond that, there's not much to it.''

''Maybe I don't want more.''

''You don't believe that any more than I do.'' He took her hands, setting them on the moist, pliant clay. ''You were born to create, Eleanor. How can you deny that portion of your soul?''

She wrenched free, putting some space between them by feeling her way along the table.

''You think you have all the answers, don't you? Give the poor little blind girl something to do with her hands and she'll live happily ever after.''

He reached her in two steps and shook her by the shoulders. ''The only one who thinks you're a 'poor little blind girl' is you. The only person feeling sorry for you is yourself.''

She drew back her hand, slapping him, her aim incredibly accurate. When he didn't release her, she wilted.

''You're right,'' she admitted softly, then laughed ruefully to herself. ''The last few days, I've been complimenting myself on how my life has returned to normal. But it isn't true. You've been right all along. I live alone in my apartment, make my way to and from work and then…nothing.''

''Don't you see? It's all a matter of choices. Yes, some of your choices have been taken away, but you can change all that. The whole world is waiting for you, Eleanor. Go take it by storm.''

She gripped his arms at his fervent entreaty, then shook her head.

''It's not as easy as it sounds, Jack.''

"Why not?"

"I was good at my work. I was finally beginning to gain national and critical attention. I can't compromise what I was with what I am now."

He spread his hands over her back, drawing her close. "How can what you do be considered a compromise if you try?"

She pondered the question, then said, "It's been a long time since I had a class in sculpting. I don't know if I even remember the basics."

"So call that fancy Art Department that asked you to evaluate their textbooks. I'm sure they can get you some help."

She frowned suspiciously. "Is that how you found out what equipment to buy?"

"A very friendly student was more than happy to spend my money."

She pulled back. "I'll need a bill for everything you've purchased."

"Take it out of your first consignment check."

"What if there is no first consignment check?"

"Then I'll expect full repayment after your first year."

Still she hesitated—as if he'd led her to a precipice and had instructed her to jump. Then, she shook her head. "No. I can't."

"Dammit, why not?"

"Because part of being an artist is reproducing life."

"Not life. Art is an impression of life as the artist interprets it to be."

He dragged her to the table and forced her hands into the soft clay.

"Show me what you see with your fingertips. Show me the things that as a sighted person I will never understand."

When she didn't move, he brought her hands up to his face and smeared the damp mud over his cheeks.

"You read countless bits of information with your fingers every single day. Why is it so difficult to think that the same lines and planes you absorb can be transferred into clay?"

Her expression remained militant.

"Do it!" he exclaimed, impatiently. "After all you've been through, all the challenges you've met and conquered, this one should be the least of your troubles. A part of your soul is aching to create. Let it go. You've brought every other aspect of your old life into play but this one. Don't cheat yourself. Don't cheat me."

Her brows drew together, her forehead creasing.

"Why is this so important to you, Jack?"

He grew very still. So many times in the past few days, he'd asked himself the same question. Now that Eleanor demanded an answer, he wasn't sure that he had one to give.

"Well?" she demanded. "Why are you always pushing me?"

"I want you to excel."

"Why?"

"Because I care for you, dammit," he exclaimed—and once the words were said, he wondered why they'd been so difficult to utter.

He *did* care for her. More than any other woman he'd ever known. She'd been the first person to touch his heart in years. And her passion! She had aroused in him a kind of desire that was white hot and immediate, yet still retained the gentler vestiges of respect, gentility, and friendship. He trusted this woman implicitly, knowing that she would never do anything to hurt him.

The thought brought a wave of shame. Unfortunately, he didn't deserve the same trust on her part. He still hadn't told her who he was.

His hands spread wide over her waist, holding her closer to him.

Now that he'd already pushed her about her art, how would she react when he told her the rest? He knew immediately that she would think he'd had some sort of ulterior motive in coming to Denver. She would probably think he'd been drawn here out of guilt or pity—and how could he make her believe any differently?

"Jack?"

His thoughts came to a screeching halt, and he remembered where he was, what he'd just admitted.

"What's the matter?" she asked quietly. "Are you regretting what you said?"

He shook his head, knowing that he would never forget this moment, never forget the way the light played over her upturned face.

"No," he replied huskily. "I'm not regretting

what I said." He touched her cheek, her lips, her nose. "I love you, Eleanor Rappaport."

Her breath hitched in her throat. "What?"

"I love you."

"But—"

"But what?" he asked teasingly.

"But you hardly know me."

"I've known you for a very long time." He couldn't hide the tinge of sadness that emerged. Knowing that he had to tell her everything now, before he lost the nerve, he said, "Eleanor, I—"

"You love me?" she breathed, interrupting him.

"Is that so surprising?"

"Yes, I—"

"Why, because you're blind?"

"No." She shook her head. "You've already proven to me time and time again that my blindness doesn't matter to you." Her fingers moved over his face, leaving fresh paths of clay. "I just didn't dare hope that you could feel the same way about me as I feel about you. I love you, too, Jack MacAllister."

The import of her words had barely managed to sink into his brain before she was drawing his head down. Rising on tiptoe, she found his mouth with unerring accuracy.

Her kiss was hot and passionate and eager, and whatever thoughts he'd been entertaining scattered from Jack's head. All he knew was this moment, this woman, this kiss.

And the fact that she loved him.

She loved him!

His arms swept around her waist, and he lifted

her to him, crushing her body into his own. Then, of their own volition his feet began making their way to the leather sofa that she had helped him to choose.

Setting her on the soft cushions, he dropped beside her, raining kisses on her cheeks, her lips, her neck.

She shuddered in delight, and he reveled in the reflex. She was so beautiful to him, so intoxicating, that he didn't know how much longer he could contain himself.

When she pushed him away, he took a deep drag of the cool air in the hopes that he could dampen his ardor.

"Jack?"

"Mmm-hmm?" He fought to pull his thoughts and his body into line. Now wasn't the time for such displays of passion. Eleanor was due anyday and...

"Jack, I think you'd better call the doctor."

In an instant his head cleared, and reality rushed into focus.

"What's wrong?"

She grinned at him. "Nothing. But my water just broke, so I think we'd better start thinking about getting me to the hospital sometime soon."

Chapter Thirteen

Eric Jackson Rappaport was born thirteen hours later, with Eleanor's mother serving as her delivery coach while Jack, Minnie and Maude paced the waiting-room carpet.

The moment Jack was told that he could visit Eleanor and the baby, he jogged down the hall and into the birthing room.

In all his life, he would never forget the sight of Eleanor propped up in bed, her face flushed with exhaustion and pride.

"Come see him, Jack," she whispered when she heard the door open.

He needed no second urging but strode to her side, his eyes devouring the sight of the wriggling bundle she held.

"A boy," he breathed. "I told you it would be a boy."

She laughed in delight. "Yes. You did."

Hesitantly he reached out a finger to touch the baby's cheek, and as if recognizing the deep boom of Jack's voice, the baby turned toward him, eyes blinking.

"He's beautiful, Eleanor."

Her eyes filled with tears of joy and regret. "I can't wait to see him. Six weeks seems suddenly so far away."

He didn't lose the import of her words. "You're going through with the surgery then?"

"As soon as possible."

"Good."

He gingerly sat on the bed beside her. "He looks like you, Eleanor. Same blue eyes."

"All babies have blue eyes."

"Not deep and dark and pansy colored."

Her smile was warm and proud.

Jack dared to slip the blue stocking cap away from the baby's brow, revealing a thick tuft of dark brown hair. "And he's got your coloring—although he looks as though he's wearing a bit of dandelion fluff at the moment."

"That's hair, Jack MacAllister."

His heart flip-flopped in delight at her indulgent, loving tone. Bending low, he brushed a kiss over Eleanor's lips.

"Congratulations," he murmured, suddenly assailed by a hunger to belong to this scene, truly belong to it. He wanted to be more than Eleanor's friend, more than her "boyfriend." He wanted to be her husband and the father to her baby.

Grinning, he took a deep, fortifying breath, knowing that the time had come for some serious "wooing."

One way or another, it was time to put all of his cards on the table and see what happened.

OVER THE NEXT FEW WEEKS life became a blur of sensation to Eleanor. Soon she was ensconced in her apartment with the baby and more help than she could ever want. Indeed, with her mother, her land-ladies, Babs and acquaintances from the art depart-ment, she often longed for time alone with Eric and Jack.

Eric was a good baby. He loved to sleep and eat and take his baths, and Eleanor was grateful. Al-though she had prepared herself and her surround-ings as much as possible for the arrival of her new baby, it wasn't until she arrived home with his warm little body cradled in her arms that she realized just how humbling it was to be responsible for another life. Despite the help offered her by her friends and relatives, *she* wanted to be the one who cared for him.

Now, more than ever before, she found herself chafing against the limitations of her blindness. She wanted to *see* Eric. She wanted to watch him grow, track his movements, monitor every nuance of his expression.

As much as possible, she Brailled Eric's little face, his hands, each curve and indentation of his body, but it wasn't the same as actually seeing him. She grew to rely on Jack's daily descriptions, as well as her mother's, but she wanted so much more for her and her son. Even if the operations failed, at least she could say she'd made every effort, tried every avenue of hope.

In the meantime, she knew she was in danger of becoming too overprotective. She carried Eric or wore him in a snuggly harness against her chest. At his slightest movement, she offered a kiss, words of praise or a soothing caress. And even though she had volunteers coming out of the woodwork to help, she had yet to spend anytime away from him—and Jack was nearly as bad as she was in that respect.

Even though Jack had moved into the loft, he was in and out of town more than he would have liked. The demands of his job were heating up, and he was on location as much as he was in Denver. But on those evenings when he was home, they spent the time together with the baby. In doing so, their relationship adopted a closeness that Eleanor would have never believed possible with another human being. For all intents and purposes, they were a family. Yet, even though she knew that Jack would like nothing more than to make such an arrangement permanent, she wasn't ready to take any lasting steps.

For one thing, there was the matter of her surgery. Although her doctor had assured her that there was nothing to worry about—and that her stay in the hospital would be minimal—she would only be allowed to have one eye at a time corrected. The procedure would take time, and it would be anyone's guess as to how much of her sight might be restored.

Yet, if she were totally honest with herself, it wasn't her blindness that scared her. She already knew that Jack loved her. No, what caused her to balk at a permanent relationship was his job. No matter how much she tried to assure herself that Jack was a professional and able to take care of himself, she still feared for his safety. How much more afraid would she be if they were to marry and he legally adopted little Eric.

"Hello, Babs."

Eleanor raised her head when she heard Jack's voice at the front of the theater. Earlier, despite Eleanor's protests, her mother had "kidnapped" the baby to show him off to her canasta group. After going to her obstetrician for her six-week checkup, Eleanor had come to The Flick for a few hours to help Barbara with inventory. But since the task was finished and her mother would have the baby for several more hours, she'd been debating what to do with the rest of her day.

Trust Jack to somehow read her thoughts.

"What are you doing here?" she asked when a hint of his cologne signalled his arrival and he bent to kiss her lips.

"I've come to take you out for the afternoon."

"Out? You took the baby and I out to dinner last night."

"Yes." He took the broom from her hands, then tugged her toward him. "But this time, I'm *really* taking you out. As in outside."

A frisson of exhilaration skittered through her body before she had the wherewithal to stop it. As much as she loved little Eric, there was something wonderful about having a few hours completely alone with Jack.

"I don't remember you ever asking me to go anywhere with you today."

"That is correct. I knew if I asked, you would say no. That's why I arranged for your mother to take Eric to her canasta tournament."

"*You* arranged that?"

"Mmm-hmm." He was still tugging her resolutely down the corridor of The Flick.

"I *should* say no," she insisted. "After all, Mother will be back soon and—"

"I thought I just explained all that. I arranged for your mother's baby-sitting services, so she is well aware of how long we'll be gone."

"I can *still* say no."

"I don't think so."

The door opened, and she was drawn into the warmth of the afternoon.

"Why not?"

"Because I have a surprise planned in your honor."

She was immediately suspicious. "What kind of surprise?"

"Something wonderful."

Digging her heels into the pavement, she refused to budge.

"I'm not going anywhere with you until you explain exactly where you plan to take me."

He sighed, then said, "Away from the city to a place where the air is incredibly clean and there's not a man-made sound for miles."

Her nose wrinkled as she considered his offer.

"How long will we be gone?" she demanded. "Eric—"

"Eric will be fine. And why does it matter where I take you? Do you have somewhere else to go?"

No. But she still balked at the idea of being away from her son any longer than necessary.

"I'm a busy mother," she said instead.

"Point taken." He curved her hand around his elbow. "I promise to have you back before dark."

She rolled her eyes at that comment. As if she would know such a detail unless she had access to a clock.

Jack leaned down, his lips brushing across her ear.

"Come on, Eleanor," he coaxed. "Take a chance. Live dangerously." Then even more softly, he said, "Trust me."

Trust him?

She did trust him. Implicitly.

"Do you plan on throwing in some dinner sometime before you bring me home?"

"Sure."

"All right, then. I'll go."

He chuckled softly, leading her to the curb and opening the car door for her. As she slid inside, she thought she imagined him saying, "As if you had a choice," before he shut her inside the vehicle.

Within moments the engine revved to life, and the car pulled into traffic.

Leaning forward, Eleanor felt for the buttons on the dashboard, finally locating the one for the radio. Immediately the air was filled with a crescendo of classical music.

"An interesting choice," she commented.

"What did you expect? Iron Butterfly?"

She thought for a moment, then said, "No, I would have pegged you as…"

"Rap?"

"Hardly."

"Country?"

"Not in the least. No, you strike me as someone who would appreciate Jazz."

There was a long silence, and she took the opportunity to punch one of the selection buttons. When the honey-rich sound of a saxophone playing the blues melted around her, she laughed in delight, settling back in her seat.

"So you think you have me figured out, hmm?"

"Not completely."

"What have you decided about my character so far?"

She thought for a moment, then answered, "You're determined, stubborn, opinionated—"

"Hey!"

"Witty, ambitious and kind."

"Kind, huh?"

She could nearly see his smug grin.

"Sometimes."

He snorted at her sassy retort. "So if you have me figured out so well, where am I taking you now?"

"Well…I'd say you've planned some idyllic setting, a picnic basket, a bottle of wine. Am I right?"

"Nope."

The car made a sharp turn, and her brow creased

when she caught the unmistakable sound of tires crunching over loose gravel.

"Where are we going?"

"I told you. Someplace remote."

She lapsed into silence, trying to piece together the sounds she heard and pinpoint her destination. When she heard the distant drone of engines, she said, "You've brought me to Denver International?"

"Not quite. It's a small commercial airport."

For the life of her, she couldn't fathom why.

"What do you intend to do? Take me across state lines?"

"Not this time."

"*This* time?" she echoed, but the car drew to a halt in a sputter of gravel, drowning out her words.

Jack quickly cut off the engine, then climbed from the car. Eleanor could hear him speaking to someone, but was unable to roll the electric windows down in order to catch the conversation more clearly.

Finally Jack opened her own door and helped her to alight.

"How was your doctor's appointment?"

"Fine. He gave me a clean bill of health."

"I know."

She paused. "You know. How?"

"I called him. I wanted to get the okay for our little adventure today. I also called your ophthalmologist. Since your surgery could be scheduled anytime a donor is located, I didn't want to do anything without his permission."

She frowned. "Exactly what have you got in mind? And why would you need my doctors to approve?"

"Let's go."

"Where are we going?"

"Dive school."

She stopped in her tracks, sure she'd heard incorrectly.

"Where?"

"Diving school. We'll be doing a tandem jump, but I'd like you to make some practice landings before we take off."

Her mouth dropped. "Jump? Landings?" Finally it dawned on her exactly what he meant. "We're at a *sky*diving school?"

"That's what I just said."

Her stomach immediately clenched, and she realized she'd told him once that she'd briefly toyed with the idea of skydiving before she'd lost her sight.

"Oh, no," she stated firmly. "I am not going to do it. I am not going to strap a parachute to my back and jump from a plane."

She whirled, stomping back in the direction of the car.

"Why not?" Jack called after her.

She spun to face him, stabbing the air with her finger. "Because it's a stupid idea, that's why!"

"What makes you say that?"

"Because I can't see, remember?" The comment was made in the same way she might point out a difficult concept to a child.

"So what? I told you we'd be jumping tandem. I'll let you know when we're about to land."

"Dammit, I am not about to—"

"I dare you."

The words were spoken so softly, so insistently, that they stopped her in midtirade.

"I dare you to do it, Eleanor," he murmured again, his boots crunching on the path as he moved toward her. "I dare you to take a chance. I dare you to prove to me—and to yourself—that you have the guts to fulfill one of your wildest fantasies."

Her hands balled into fists. "I will not let you bully me into breaking my neck. I'm a mother, for Heaven's sake. I have to be responsible."

"You won't break your neck. I'll make sure you don't."

"How are you going to prevent a mishap?"

"I do this sort of thing for a living, remember? Your safety is my first priority."

His voice enfolded her like a silken cocoon. To her horror, she found herself hesitating.

"Do it, Eleanor. If you agree it will be the thrill of a lifetime. If your refuse, you'll always wonder what it would have been like. You'll regret having said no. I promise you."

"Dammit, Jack," she whispered, torn between her innate caution and her pride. He was right in one respect. If she buckled beneath his dare, she would be furious with herself.

But if she accepted the challenge, she would be jumping from a plane. She would be leaping into nothingness with only this man to keep her out of harm's way.

"Trust me, Eleanor," he said again, his fingers stroking her cheek. "I won't disappoint you."

No. He wouldn't. She knew that deep in her heart. All that remained was for her to find the courage not to disappoint herself.

"What if I throw up?" she muttered.

"I won't tell a soul."

"What if I faint?"

"You won't faint."

"What if I scream?"

He chuckled. "Are you planning to inventory every possible reaction? If so, there's no way I'll get you home by dark."

When she didn't respond he bent to brush his lips over hers.

"What's your answer, Eleanor?"

Sighing, she closed her eyes, knowing that she'd completely lost her mind.

"All right. Let's go."

For hours a gruff-voiced man named One-Eye drilled Eleanor on all the skills she needed for the tandem jump. Jack had introduced One-Eye as a close friend and had told her the man would be going with them as an added safety measure—as well as to film the jump for her to enjoy once she'd had her surgery.

Eleanor was touched by the gesture—as well as by the tacit faith Jack seemed to have in the transplant's success. It was as if he took it for granted that she would see again. Soon. She drew great comfort from his attitude and even began mugging to One-Eye's efforts behind the camera. Someday, Eric would watch the video as well, and she wanted visual proof of her daring feat.

She also grew to like One-Eye immediately. He was witty and cantankerous—often goading Jack into laughter. It was obvious that he cared for Jack a great deal and he felt Eleanor brought his friend great joy. At one time he even reassured her that she was lucky to be jumping with "Jack Man," the best in the business. But before she could inquire about the nickname, Jack took her hand and led her to the waiting plane.

Her heart pounded so hard in her chest, she feared it would escape.

"Maybe this isn't such a good idea," she muttered to no one in particular.

"What?" Jack shouted over the roar of the plane's engine.

She tugged on his hand, forcing him to stop. Around her, she heard the chatter of the other student jumpers as they hurried to take their places.

"Jack, are you sure this is a good idea?"

"You don't want to back out now, do you?"

"No, but I—"

He cupped her cheeks in his hands. "You'll do great. Remember, I'll do most of the hard stuff. All you have to do is relax and enjoy the ride."

She wasn't so sure how much "enjoying" she would be able to manage, but she summoned a weak grin nevertheless. If the past few hours had taught her nothing else, they'd helped her to see that—as crazy as the notion sounded—she actually *wanted* to make the jump. She wanted to prove to herself that she was still young and vital, that she still had the guts to try something new and different.

Added to that was the fact that she wanted to show Jack she was capable of performing a daring escapade every now and then.

"Let's go."

He gave her hand a reassuring squeeze, then directed her up the narrow stairs that led into the fuselage of the plane. Once inside, she took her place on a hard, narrow bench, and focused on her breathing.

Relax.

Over and over again, Jack and One-Eye had insisted that relaxing was one of the primary rules for success in any jump.

But how could she relax when her heart was thumping like the rhythm section of a marching band?

Jack slung his arm around her shoulders and she willingly sank against his body, her fingers curling tightly around the edge of her seat.

"You don't need to hang on yet, we won't be leaving for a few minutes."

"How can you be so calm?"

"This is old hat to me, remember?"

"How can jumping out of a plane ever become old hat?"

She felt him shrug, then the engine revved, the metal plates beneath her feet vibrating with energy.

Taking a deep breath, Eleanor grabbed Jack's thigh, her fingers holding onto him for dear life. Bit by bit, she felt the plane gathering speed until it hurtled down the runway. Then, the nose tipped up, the wheels bounced ever so slightly, and she knew they were airborne.

Several moments later, she became conscious of the hard muscle she gripped, and she winced.

"You must think I'm some sort of hysterical female."

His fingers stroked her neck. "Not at all. In fact I envy you."

"Envy me?" she repeated in disbelief.

"Yes. This is your first time. The experience will be completely new, raw. You'll never be the same again, and no other jump will ever be so terrifying and energizing."

A dryness entered her mouth. Something about his explanation seemed to carry a much more subtle image. One that was completely sensual.

Intimate.

"I'm proud of you, Eleanor," Jack said lowly, so much so that she nearly didn't catch the words. But as a warmth flooded her limbs and the last of her fears subsided, she was glad she'd caught them. Not since she'd been a child had anyone's approval meant this much to her.

A buzzer pierced the air.

"Time to rock and roll," Jack said.

"What about the other students?"

"You and I will be jumping over a different target. After all, you're blind. We wouldn't want you bumping into any of the novices, would we?''

"Very funny."

"I thought so."

Eleanor slid her helmet over her head, tightened the strap beneath her chin and slid her goggles into place. After checking and rechecking her harness, Jack helped her up.

"Ready?"

She knew if she tried to speak, her words would emerge as an incomprehensible bleat, so she nodded.

"Remember to stay loose. Let me do all the work."

Again she nodded.

Positioning her back to his chest, he clipped their harnesses together.

"Let's go."

His thighs pushed at hers as he led her to the door. All at once she felt a cool draft of air pressing against her, urging her to remain inside the plane. But she ignored the idea of surrendering to her own misgivings. Not this time.

Jack braced his arms on either side of the doorway.

"Ready?"

Her head bobbed.

"On three."

The wind rushed over her face, chilling her cheeks.

"One."

Dear, sweet Heaven above, she was going to do it. She was going to jump from a plane.

"Two."

"If we don't make it, I want you to know I had a wonderful time today, Jack."

He laughed. "We'll make it. Three!"

Then they were leaping into nothingness. Eleanor squealed as her stomach lurched into her throat as if she'd descended the hill of an immense roller-coaster ride. Overhead she heard the plane roar past them, then fade away.

"Are we falling?" she called out over the rush of air.

"Yes."

"Is One-Eye following?"

"He's right behind us."

Eleanor became aware of the way Jack's arms had wound about her waist.

"Shouldn't you be pulling the chute?"

"Not yet."

"But—"

She felt his cheek press against hers. "We're flying, Eleanor. We don't want to give up the sensation too soon."

She became still as she realized the sinking sensation had disappeared. Indeed, if not for the wind whistling past her ears, she might have thought they were floating instead of rushing toward the ground.

Laughing, Jack shifted, causing them to twist and turn in a series of aeronautic acrobatics. At first Eleanor clung to him, trying not to think of how quickly they must be succumbing to gravity's force. But then, as Jack's aura of confidence seeped into her body, she surrendered to him, laughing in triumph.

She'd done it! She'd actually jumped from a plane!

"Geronimo!" she shouted into the wind and space and silence.

"Hang on."

Within seconds of his warning, she heard the ripping sound of the chute being released. She was tugged upward by her harness straps as if they'd been yanked by an unseen hand. Overhead, she noted the ruffle and flap of the shute as it unfurled and caught the air. Then she and Jack were floating through the air, lazily, like a pair of autumn leaves.

"This is wonderful!" she cried out.

Jack's own laughter was just as contagious. "I knew you'd like it."

"I'm so glad you brought me."

"Kidnapped you, don't you mean?"

"Whatever."

Suddenly it didn't matter that he'd brought her to this point under the guise of a simple outing. "I really underestimated you."

"In what way?"

"I had this whole day out pegged as a picnic."

Again he chuckled. "Actually, there's a picnic basket and a bottle of wine waiting for us at our destination."

She grinned. "Perfect. I'm in the mood for a celebration."

Jack's hands rubbed over her midriff. "You are, hmm?"

"Yes."

"Provided we don't break any bones landing, you mean."

"It won't matter. I'll still want to celebrate."

"Good. Because we're about a hundred yards from the ground."

Eleanor lapsed into silence, allowing Jack to release her and concentrate on maneuvering them both into an optimum position for landing.

"Stay relaxed and focused," he offered quickly, and she knew it wouldn't be long. "Keep your knees bent, and remember to drop and roll if you don't hit feet first."

She nodded to show she'd understood, while every sense became more attuned to her surroundings. Straining, she wondered if she would be able to hear the grass and rock and earth just before they hit.

"Fifty feet," Jack called out.

How far was that? Two stories? Three?

"Twenty."

Relax. Knees bent.

"Now!"

All too soon she felt the soles of her boots slam into the dirt. Her knees immediately reacted, bending at the same moment that Jack's arm swept around her waist and he half lifted, half pushed her a dozen steps until he'd gained his balance. Then he stopped, still standing, and the parachute sighed softly, collapsing to the ground.

For several long minutes Eleanor remained completely still and silent. Vaguely she felt him unstrapping her harness and releasing his own. Not allowing him to tend to the parachute, she whirled and threw her arms around his neck, hugging him tightly.

"Thank you!" she whispered fervently.

Tilting her head a fraction of an inch, she covered his lips, kissing him with all the fervor and excitement that had built to a fever pitch in her body.

Perhaps it was the brush with danger she'd experienced, or the thrill of adventure, but he tasted that much better, felt that much harder. She pressed tighter and tighter to his body, needing to absorb each nuance of his form so that she would never forget this moment as long as she lived.

Never forget this passion.

Never forget this man.

"I want to make love to you, Jack," she sighed against him.

He groaned, kissing her again. But their intimacy was shattered when One-Eye shouted, "Hey! Was that a perfect jump or what?"

Eleanor jerked free as she heard the thump of One-Eye's boots hitting the earth, then the flap and flutter of his parachute. But when Eleanor would have stepped away, Jack took her hand.

"We're going home," he murmured, "as soon as I can get us out of here. Then I plan to take you up on your offer."

Eleanor shivered in delight and anticipation.

Finally.

Finally she would know what it was like to make love to him.

Chapter Fourteen

Jack had packed the picnic in the trunk of the car, but at her insistence, they left One-Eye at the target area and made their way home to her apartment.

Issuing orders for him to assemble the picnic upstairs, she hurried into the bathroom, ran a comb through her hair, then paused to stare in the direction of the mirror.

If her sight were to be magically restored, she wondered what she would see there. Would her eyes sparkle in triumph or desire…

…or love?

She loved Jack MacAllister, heart and soul. There was no avoiding the truth any longer. And although she still had qualms about his job, their skydiving adventure had taught her that Jack was very careful, very knowledgeable and very experienced.

But was experience enough to ward off disaster?

Pushing that thought away, she climbed the steps to the loft, knowing that the time had come for her to bring their relationship to another, higher level. He'd been living above her apartment for weeks, torturing her with his nearness. And as the promise of sensual fulfillment flooded her veins with a silken heat, she grew inestimably impatient.

"I'm over here."

His voice offered her the direction she needed to find him in the velvety darkness. And as soon as she'd come close enough, he grasped her hand, pulling her down to him, kissing her with a passion that neither could deny.

"You are so beautiful," Jack gasped at one point, breaking away so that they could both take deep gulps of air.

Eleanor smiled against his cheek, then his chest. Then she drew back to whip her T-shirt over her head.

Jack gasped, surprised by her boldness as well as by the sight that awaited him.

What Eleanor was wearing should have been considered illegal. If he'd known that her breasts had been contained by mere wisps of lace, he knew that he wouldn't have been able to keep his hands off her as long as he had.

Her fingers began working at the buttons of his shirt.

"Take this off."

Jack cleared his throat to attempt to alleviate the sensual tension that gripped him.

"Are you sure that's wise?"

"It is if we're going to make love." Her smile was tender, rueful. "That is what we're going to do, isn't it?"

"I don't know," he muttered, and she laughed.

"Come now, Jack. You've been downright bossy in every other respect. You've already conspired with my doctors, my mother and probably my land-ladies. Surely you haven't lost your nerve."

Offering him a mischievous look, she tugged at the placket of his shirt, causing the buttons to pop and scatter over the hardwood floor in a muted chatter. Then she was drawing him down for her kiss.

The moment the flesh of his chest touched her own, he was lost. He couldn't have drawn back now if a gun had been put to his head.

She loved him.

She wanted to make love with him.

Then there was no thought for anything but the passion roaring inside him and the sweet torment of her embrace. He reveled in each caress of her hands, those delicate, eloquent hands. When she lay back, taking him with her, he gasped in raw pleasure as their bodies rubbed.

Kiss by kiss she showed him how much she cared for him, and when the time came for their bodies to become one, he groaned in sheer delight, never having known how love could make this ritual so much more heady, so much more powerful.

Moving against her, he brought Eleanor to her release, and then, when he took his own, he leaned close and whispered, "I love you so much."

She gazed up at him with tear-filled eyes.

"I know. I know. Just as I love you."

THE NEXT FEW WEEKS PASSED in a haze of excitement and desire. Since she'd taken an extended leave of absence from The Flick, she spent her days with the baby. And while Eric napped, she indulged herself in her workroom, her hands twisting and molding the clay.

She hadn't realized how much her soul had hungered for an artistic outlet until she'd made love with Jack in this room. Then, as if her dam had been broken, she'd found herself needing to express herself with her art.

Not that the transition to clay had been an easy one. The first afternoon she'd forced herself to climb to the attic, she'd told herself that she would give the enterprise one hour. If she couldn't summon any enthusiasm for the medium, she would tell Jack to go to the devil if need be.

But that hour had stretched into five, then six. The hours weren't completely uninterrupted, of course. Eric was still at an age where he napped a great deal. But whenever he was awake, she would take a break and play silly baby games or simply cuddle him and hum. But the moment he fell asleep again, she invariably found herself drawn back to her work table.

Since that first day she'd spent untold hours with her sculptures. When Jack was away during the week on a shooting assignment, she missed him horribly, but in a way she was slightly relieved. His absence allowed her to learn to work with the clay without an audience. And since he had moved into the main part of her apartment, the loft was her private area. She'd made her mistakes, she'd endured untold frustration, but at long last she was beginning to enjoy the pieces she created—so much so that she wondered why she'd never tried sculpting before. Working with the cool, wet clay, feeling it absorb the heat of her hands, was a completely sensual experience. One that she found to be—in many ways—much more satisfying and liberating than her painting had ever been.

She'd already begun making plans. Since she and Jack had finally finished their evaluation of the textbooks, she'd refused any sort of payment and had asked instead for an exchange of services. Her expertise had been traded for the instructional aid of a graduate student who helped her assemble the metal armatures she needed as support beneath the clay sculptures. In time she hoped to become experienced enough to make them herself, but she knew such challenges would have to wait until she grew more familiar with the new medium.

''Eleanor!''

The call came from downstairs, and Eleanor supported the baby's head as she hopped off the high stool where she'd perched to work on a bust of the very man who called her. Eric had grown accustomed to being in the baby harness she often wore as she worked. He cooed in obvious delight at the sound of Jack's voice. At two months, he was growing more and more aware of his surroundings and the people who adored him. Jack was a particular favorite and Eric kicked and squealed whenever he heard him. The baby clearly anticipated the tickles and ''guy games'' Jack claimed were good for growing boys.

Dropping a plastic bag over the top of the unfinished head, she called, "Up here!"

Immediately her pulse leaped, and her stomach made excited flip-flops. Jack had been out of town for more than five days, and she'd been half listening for the door for more than an hour.

But her steps slowed as she realized that it was not one set of footsteps coming up the stairs, but two.

Unsure who might be accompanying Jack she went to the sink, washed her hands, then carefully removed the baby from the harness. After dropping the harness on the couch, she tucked Eric into her arm and turned just as Jack and his guest entered the room.

"Hey, Eric!"

The baby burbled excitedly and kicked. An instant later, Eric was taken from her arms and Jack brushed his lips over hers.

"Hi," he said for her ears alone. Then he turned toward the room.

"Wow," Jack breathed.

She smiled, knowing that he was studying the half dozen sculptures lining the room.

"Do you like them?"

"Yes, I do."

The voice that answered her was unfamiliar, and she frowned.

"Eleanor, this is Martin Scaparelli."

Her brows rose. "Aren't you the owner of—"

"Scaparelli Galleries," the man said, "here in Denver."

She walked toward the sound of his voice, holding out her hand.

Martin vigorously shook it, then turned, presumably to study the pieces. "These are really marvelous, Miss Rappaport."

Eleanor was still unsure why this man was here, but she managed a bemused, "Thank you."

Jack took her hand, his fingers twining with hers.

"Scaparelli is an advisor for one of the scenes we had to reshoot."

"An art advisor for a techno-thriller?" she asked dubiously.

Martin gave a bark of laughter. "Go figure, eh?"

"We ate lunch a couple of times, and your name came up."

"Oh, really," Eleanor drawled, clearly suspicious.

Martin chuckled. "He said you wouldn't believe our meeting was merely by chance."

Jack squeezed her hand. "Honest. We were just talking."

"I'm a big fan of yours, Miss Rappaport," Martin said, his voice floating around the room as he continued his exploration. "I bought several of your earlier works—and one of your murals is located in a park just outside my front door."

Eleanor felt a tingle of excitement. She knew the precise mural he was talking about—only one of many that she'd created as part of her graduate project.

"It's nice to know my work is still remembered," she said, pleased.

"Remembered! When I heard about your accident, I was distraught. I'd already begun to approach your agent about a showing."

"Really?"

"Yes. I'd hoped to get an acceptance to my offer before your exhibition at the National Gallery. After that, I figured you would be hot property."

Eleanor shifted, disconcerted by the man's open flattery. "Are you sure Jack didn't pay you to say all these things?"

Martin laughed. "I'm sure. As a matter of fact, Miss Rappaport, I've been seeking new artists for a special show I've arranged. I've signed everyone I need, but..."

Eleanor felt a strange tingling begin in the ends of her fingers and instantly recognized the feeling as anticipation.

"After coming here, I believe I've found one that *must* be included."

Eleanor automatically gripped Jack's hand even tighter, feeling her knees go weak. "You can't be serious."

"I'm very serious."

"But I've only been working in this medium for a short time."

"I'll be honest with you, Eleanor. A few of your pieces are rough."

Her stomach knotted in response, even though she knew he was right—and she valued his honesty.

"Nevertheless, there is a raw eloquence to your work that I think will translate both critically and commercially."

Eleanor licked her lips, wondering how she should respond.

"Are you still with the same agent?"

"I've kept in contact with her, but since I haven't worked in over a year..." She left the rest of the statement hanging.

"I'll get in touch with her." She heard the rustling of his clothes and the click of a retracting ballpoint pen. "Here's my card."

Eleanor automatically reached for it, even though her limbs had grown numb.

"The showing will be the first week of July."

"July!" But that was less than a month away.

"I'd like you to develop a dozen or so pieces, then I'll choose from the cream of the crop."

"Fine."

"Keep in mind that you'll be one of eight other artists."

She nodded to show she understood.

"But, if all goes well, I'd like to schedule you for a solo showing next year some time."

She was shaking so hard she feared he would see it.

"Mr. Scaparelli...are you sure about this?"

He laughed, slapping her on the shoulder as if they were old chums. "Listen to her, Jack. Am I sure? Hell, yes. Especially since I intend to make a great deal of money from your work, Eleanor. I'm not about to leave you to some other gallery." This time, the clasping of her shoulder was gentle, as if he were a doting grandfather. "Do we have a deal?"

"As long as your proposal passes my agent's inspection."

He chortled in delight, deep belly laughs that were infectious. "That'a girl! I might make a lot of money, but you're savvy enough to see to it that I don't make too much."

Taking her free hand, he shook it, then strode to the stairs. "I'll be in touch."

"Thank you, Mr. Scaparelli."

She and Jack remained completely motionless, waiting until they heard the man shut her apartment door, then shuffle down the outer entrance. At long last they heard the distant grumble of an engine.

"He's gone," Eleanor sighed.

"I suppose so. He kept our cab waiting at the corner."

Several moments passed before Eleanor began to absorb what had happened.

"He liked my work," she stated softly.

Jack squeezed her fingers.

"Are you sure you didn't put him up to this?" she asked one last time.

Lifting their joined hands, he made an *X* over his chest. "Cross my heart. Our meeting was purely by chance."

He bent and kissed her, and within seconds a familiar passion gripped them both.

Drawing away, Jack took a breath, held it, then said, "First things first. I need to say hello to Eric before this progresses any further. Then I need some food. I'm starving—I haven't eaten since sometime yesterday afternoon."

"Jack!" she protested. "That's no way to take care of yourself."

He pulled her into his arms. Eric cooed in delight, reaching to grasp at Eleanor's shirt. "I was trying to wrap up all the loose ends from the retakes so that I could get back as soon as possible."

"How long will you be able to stay?"

"Three days."

"Three days!" she echoed, horrified.

"They moved up the production schedule for my next project."

She scowled in mock ferocity. "And here I'd hoped you would be coming back for an extended period of time."

He framed her chin in his fingers. "I wish I could. Unfortunately I'll only be able to manage a few odd days in the next six weeks."

He'd become so serious she knew she'd struck a chord.

Kissing his palm, she offered lightly, "I suppose it's just as well that you won't be around much. I have work of my own to do...and so little time," she added with something akin to panic.

"Are you upset with me for bringing Scaparelli?"

"Upset? Why would I be upset?" Since Jack still held the baby, she threw her arms around his neck, hugging him tightly. "For the first time in over a year, I'm going to be showing my work."

"I'm proud of you, Eleanor," he said next to her ear, and she warmed from the inside out. His praise was in many ways as important to her as Scaparelli's confidence in her abilities.

"Thank you, Jack."

"I only brought the man home."

"You've done more than that, so much more," she whispered huskily. Then she kissed him, knowing that some emotions were better expressed in actions than in words.

OVER THE NEXT FEW WEEKS Eleanor worked feverishly to prepare for the show at the Scaparelli Gallery. Resigning from her job at The Flick, she spent every waking hour in the attic, honing skills that were still so new to her.

Her only breaks occurred when Jack was able to visit. During those times the two of them behaved like a newlywed couple escaping from humanity. They locked themselves in her apartment, doted on the baby, ordered takeout for meals or ventured out to the local eateries. They talked for hours on end, made love and inundated themselves with each other's company.

But each time he walked out the door again, Eleanor realized she still knew so little about the man. He was infinitely complex. Layered like an onion. She began to understand portions of his personality, but found more and more layers beneath.

And with each revelation, she grew to love him more completely and irrevocably.

Therein lay her problem. She should have been able to commit herself wholeheartedly to this man. She'd already declared her feelings for him—and with each visit his personal belongings were finding permanent places in her home. So why did she still feel a part of herself holding back?

His job.

Sighing, Eleanor tugged on the zipper of the "little black dress" she planned to wear to the opening. Now that her figure had gone back to its prepregnancy shape, she was able to squeeze into it once more.

Jack was a stuntman, just as she was an artist. It was a part of him, an elemental portion of his soul that she could not change. He loved his work and reveled in the effects he created as much as she did her sculptures.

So why couldn't she leave the whole situation alone? Why couldn't she accept that his job was dangerous, then learn to live with the fact?

Because the element of risk scared her.

She couldn't bear it if Jack were hurt—or worse yet, if he were somehow disabled as she had been. Every day she told herself that he was careful, that he was a professional. But every day she was still afraid.

Could she really live that way?

But if she couldn't, could she live without Jack?

Her head swam from her efforts to find a solution to the problem. She knew Jack sensed her reticence. She also knew that they should talk about her qualms. But whenever they were together, they invariably skirted all reference to the future, as if by ignoring such a discussion they could avert the consequences of time.

But they had to talk.

Tonight, she decided. After the opening.

Moving into the nursery at the first snuffling cries, Eleanor murmured, "Perfect timing, my little man."

She had purposely waited until the last minute to get Eric ready for the show, knowing that the minute she got him dressed in his miniature tuxedo, he would be kicking at the matching black knitted booties.

The outfit was a gift from Jack, who had proclaimed that Eric needed to dress the part for the evening. From the description Eleanor had been given, the shorts and matching jacket with "tails" were made of shiny black satin while the one-piece body suit had been fashioned to resemble a tucked shirt complete with studs and a bow tie. To this was added white ankle socks with a knitted design resembling black wing tip shoes. Then, as a crowning touch, a sterling silver pacifier pin kept Eric's beloved "binkie" close at hand.

Not for the first time, she wished she could see the results. But since Jack had been keeping a running record of Eric's growth with a video camera, she had hoped that one day soon she could compare her memories to actual events.

After quickly dressing the baby and smoothing a brush over the fluffy hair on the crown of his head, she carried Eric into the main room. Humming to him, she rocked back and forth.

Nervously popping the crystal to her wristwatch, she felt for the time and frowned in concern. Where was Jack? He'd promised to escort her to the gallery.

Moving aimlessly with the baby in her arms, she

rechecked her hair, her gown, her hosiery. Then, running out of things to do, she began to tidy an already-tidy apartment. Listlessly she flipped on the television.

"...just announced that a fire spread through one of the sound studios, critically injuring one stuntman and a grip. Back to you, Bob."

Eleanor froze, then scrambled to turn up the volume, but the announcer had already moved on to another topic. Desperate, she used the remote to flip through the channels, but the news programs failed to offer any more information that the snippet of a sentence she'd heard.

A stuntman had been injured. Critically. On a sound stage.

Where? Where?

She was pacing the area in front of her windows when Jack burst through the door.

"I'm sorry," he rushed to explain. "My plane has been circling the airport for the better part of an hour."

Eleanor was so relieved to hear his voice that she rushed toward him, hugging him tightly around the neck. When the baby squawked in protest it took all the will she possessed to loosen her hold even a little, and she couldn't prevent the sob of relief that burst from her throat.

"Hey?" Jack said in concern. "What's the matter?"

He dropped his bags to the floor with a bump and wrapped his arms around her waist.

"I was so worried."

"I'm sorry. I would have called, but the plane didn't have one of those phones and—"

"No, it's not that," she sobbed, unable to control her tears.

"Then what?"

She rested her head on his shoulders, her tears dampening the bare skin above his collar.

"Didn't you hear the news?"

"No. I've been on a plane most of the day. We had to shoot some sequences in Canada yesterday, and I didn't get a chance to let you know. I figured I'd be home today."

Home. She liked the way the word sounded on his lips.

Straightening, she wiped the tears from her face, but when she would have backed away, he pulled her close again, cradling her head against his chest.

"So what's up?"

She took a deep, ragged breath. "There was an accident at one of the movie studios. I heard just a snippet of the story and I...I..."

She began crying again, and he held her tightly, rocking her.

"Have you been watching trash television again?"

"What do you mean?"

"I think the story you're talking about was the fire on one of the Universal sets. One of their stunt-men was injured slightly, but I've heard through the grapevine that he's already out of the hospital. A few of the tabloid television programs have been blowing the whole event out of proportion."

"I thought it was you," she whispered hoarsely. "I thought *you'd* been hurt."

She was afraid that he would tease her for her silly fears, but he grew quite still, quite serious.

"My work bothers you, doesn't it?"

She nodded against him. "I can't help it. I've told myself time and time again that I have no right to worry."

"No right?" he interrupted. "I think you have every right. I would be more worried about you if you *didn't* worry."

She couldn't help laughing. "That doesn't make any sense."

"Maybe the words themselves don't, but the meaning behind them is as plain as day. I like the fact that you worry about me. I like knowing that you're waiting for my call at the end of the day. I like the way you drop everything when I come to visit because you know I can't stay as long as I wish I could."

He cupped her face, lifting her head, and she knew he was studying her, just as her own hands had unconsciously lifted to his cheeks to read his expression.

"In the past few weeks I've developed quite a reputation for myself. I've always been careful, but now I check every detail of a stunt again and again because I know how much my work disturbs you. I don't want to do anything that would upset you even more, let alone hurt myself. If I did that, you'd never forgive me."

Her lips trembled, then drew into an unwilling smile. "You're right. I wouldn't."

"I'm also arranging to cut back on my work."

"What?" she breathed.

"I couldn't do anything about this current project, because I was already committed. In the past I've filled every minute of the day with work." He stroked her lips. "Now I have one or two more important items requiring my time." His body grew tense. "But if I'm assuming too much, making too many demands, let me know."

She shook her head. "You aren't assuming too much."

"Good." He took the baby from her arms. "Because I have something else I need to get off my chest—"

"No more talking."

"But Eleanor..."

"We'll talk later," she said firmly, then wrapped her arms around his waist. "Right now I want you to reassure me that all of your parts are in perfect working order."

IT WAS SOMETIME LATER before they tucked Eric in his carrier and hurried downstairs to knock on Minnie and Maude's door.

"Eleanor! My lands, I thought you two would never be ready," Maude grumbled. "Minnie must have called upstairs three times. Have you got your phone turned off again?"

Jack felt a slight tinge of heat seep into his

cheeks. "My fault. I think I bumped the outlet with my suitcase."

Maude shot him a disbelieving glance. "Mmm." Then she bellowed, "Minnie, move your bustle. Time's awasting! We've got to get to Eleanor's opening!"

When they arrived a crowd had already gathered to see the artists who were being featured. Eleanor was immediately hustled away by Martin, and Jack stood back, watching her.

She appeared so different from the way she'd been that first time he'd seen her walking in the rain. She radiated confidence and vitality—a far cry from the woman who had jumped at unfamiliar noises.

"Jack?"

Taking one of the flutes of champagne from a passing waiter, Jack found Minnie and Maude standing behind him.

Both women had dressed with great care for the evening—Maude in her finest support shoes and hose and a severe gray suit. Minnie, being much more flamboyant than her older sister, wore a dress made of tier upon tier of exotic organza ruffles. Even Regina, who had arrived at the opening mere minutes before the rest of the group, was regally decked out in her finest. Playing the proud grandmother, she was escorting Eric from one group of people to another, introducing herself and exclaiming, "That's my daughter's work!" to whoever would listen.

The chatter of the crowd flowed around Jack as he moved, but he could have been alone in the room for all the attention he gave it. He was in love, and he didn't care who knew it. He intended to slip his arm around Eleanor's waist and kiss her for all the world to see. Then, when the evening was over, he would take her home—that was what her apartment had become to him.

Home.

"Hi," he murmured, drawing her close.

She melted into him easily, contentment flooding her features. "I've sold two pieces already."

"Fantastic!" He bent to nuzzle her ear. "When we get back home, I need to talk to you," he said, knowing that his confession would have to be made. He couldn't wait any longer—he didn't want to wait any longer. It was time she knew their first meeting had been near Estes Park, not Denver. "Then, if you aren't too mad at me, I'd like to marry you."

She grew still in his arms. "What?"

"Hey, Eleanor!"

Jack frowned when Victor Russo's booming voice shattered the moment. The stuntman held a flute of champagne in one hand. A beautiful woman with an incredibly short skirt graced the other.

"It's Victor," Jack said grudgingly as the couple joined them. "We went to one of his parties."

Eleanor nodded in recognition. "Hello, Victor."

"This is quite an event. I don't think I've ever known a real artist before."

She smiled graciously, although it was obvious to everyone that Victor was slightly drunk.

"Would you like something to drink?" Jack asked Eleanor quietly.

She nodded. "A soda, please."

Excusing himself from Victor's inane prattle, Jack made his way to the buffet, selecting a chilled soda and a tiny plate of hors d'oeuvres.

As he returned he noted that Victor was gesticulating wildly, but Eleanor's features had grown tense and pale.

Dammit. Victor was probably regaling her with tales of horror about stunts gone wrong. Jack never should have left her with the man.

Moving faster, he arrived in time to hear Victor say, "...One-Eye told me about how you and Jack first met."

"Yes. He helped me do some reading."

Jack's muscles felt suddenly laden with iron. He opened his mouth to interrupt Victor, but it was already too late.

"No, not that. How he met you months earlier." Victor clucked his tongue. "Horrible. What an accident. I was working with him at the time, and I remember how shaken he was by the whole thing...."

Victor continued, but Jack wasn't listening to him any longer. The damage had been done. He saw Eleanor's features grow deathly white, and she bit her trembling lip. For an instant she stared toward him as if she could actually see, and her expression was so filled with disbelief and betrayal that Jack winced.

"Eleanor, I can explain," he said.

She jumped as if his voice was the last thing she'd expected to hear. "That was you?" she whispered. "In the pickup?"

"Yes. I meant to tell you, but whenever I started to say something, I became distracted and..."

His explanation trailed into silence.

Minnie and Maude approached, drawn by Eleanor's obvious distress.

"Are you ill, dear?" Minnie inquired.

"Yes. No, I—" Her voice grew choked and she whispered tightly. "Minnie, will you help me to the ladies' room please?"

"Of course, sweetie."

Minnie took her arm, leading Eleanor through the milling crowds.

Jack watched them go, a slow despair filling his soul. Her expression had been so eloquently wounded, he knew that she wouldn't believe his protestations now. She would think he'd purposely lied to her—or worse yet, that he'd been drawn here by guilt and that his declarations of love were feigned.

Turning, he woodenly set the glass and plate on a nearby ledge, knowing that Eleanor would want him to leave this way. Quietly. Without a fuss. After all, he'd already ruined her special night.

And she would never believe him.

Never.

"Jack?" he heard Regina call behind him. "Jack!"

Opening the door of the gallery, he stepped into the darkness without saying goodbye.

Chapter Fifteen

Eleanor ran her hands under the cool water, trying to block out the images that flooded her brain. A slick road, a web of cracked glass.

Then a face.

Dark hair.

Dark eyes.

Jack.

Jack had been the one to draw her out of the car when the smell of gasoline had grown too intense and the threat of an explosion had become imminent. Jack had been the one to carry her to safety, lay her on the ground and cradle her in his arms. She remembered how strong he'd been. How he'd offered her a litany of comforting words.

Then the light had dimmed and grown black.

Jack MacAllister. She vaguely remembered her mother referring to that name when Eleanor was in the hospital. But it had never occurred to Eleanor that she'd met him before. Whenever she'd found herself thinking his voice seemed familiar, she'd been sure their encounter in the Kensington Hotel lobby had been the reason.

Taking a deep breath, she lifted her wet hands to her cheeks, calming somewhat.

He must think her a ninny for growing all shaky and running away from him like a startled rabbit. She'd just been so shocked to discover that the man she had always considered to be her guardian angel on that horrible night was the same man that she loved body and soul.

Minnie patted her back. "Are you feeling better?"

"Yes. I don't know what came over me," Eleanor said, not wanting to explain what had actually occurred. She didn't wish to rehash the scene in the gallery. She needed to find Jack.

"It's probably all the excitement and the heat of the crowd," Minnie insisted. "I don't know why they invited so many people."

"If you could take me back to Jack now," Eleanor prompted.

The door squeaked. "He's gone," Maude's strident voice announced.

Eleanor grabbed a towel and dabbed at her face. "What do you mean 'he's gone?'"

"I don't have the slightest notion what happened, but when the two of you came in here, he left." She slapped her hands together. "Just like that!"

"Oh, no," Eleanor whispered, knowing instinctively that he'd thought she'd been upset by Victor's words, rather than merely surprised.

"Minnie, get a cab. We've got to go home."

''But the opening!''

''I don't care about the opening. Tell Martin I've taken ill, or...or that I've fainted. Just collect the baby and his things, then get me a cab and my purse from Martin's office.''

ELEANOR FELT as if the Fates were conspiring against her. First, her purse couldn't be found. After it had finally been located in Martin's desk drawer, an avid art collector had insisted on speaking to her. Then the cab was late, a collection of fire engines delayed their progress, and Minnie couldn't find enough change to tip the driver.

Finally Eleanor offered him one of the bills from her own wallet. According to the way she'd folded it, she knew it was a fifty, but she didn't care. She had to stop Jack before he did something stupid.

Like running.

But as soon as she entered her apartment, she knew that he'd already come and gone. A hollowness filled the air—and when she called out, no one answered.

Damn! How could he do this to her? How could he think that she would blame him for what had happened on that highway?

But even as the recrimination reverberated in her head, she knew she'd given him no reason to believe otherwise. When he'd first met her, she'd been full of anger and frustration...and yes, a good measure of self-pity. Naturally, he would assume that she still felt a portion of those emotions and that she blamed *him* for what had occurred.

"Well, he's wrong," she stated to no one in particular, striding to her room.

Calling Information, she asked for the number used to page passengers at the airport. Instinctively she knew he would be on his way back to Los Angeles. She didn't know what airline he generally used, but it didn't matter. She was going to page him until dawn if she had to.

BY NOON THE NEXT DAY Eleanor was forced to concede defeat. If Jack had gone to the airport as she'd assumed, he'd either missed her frequent pages or he had ignored them—and since the airport operator was growing testy, Eleanor was forced to try another tack.

First, she rang Martin Scaparelli in hopes that Jack had given the man his home address or phone number.

But in between telling her that all of her sculptures had sold and inquiring about her health, Martin had been unable to supply any information on Jack.

Next, she called the university's art department and volunteer services department. Neither had a California address for Jack, but the receptionist did give her Victor Russo's address.

"Mr. MacAllister was living there for a while and left the address and phone number in case we needed to contact him," the woman explained.

Hanging up the phone, Eleanor next called Regina. "Mom, I need your help...."

Within minutes Regina had closed her shop and driven to Eleanor's house.

"Here's the address," Eleanor said as she clipped the buckle to Eric's car seat, then climbed into the passenger side and handed her mother the scrap of notebook paper where she'd scribbled the information.

"My goodness," her mother said drolly. "Your handwriting's better now than when you could see."

"Very funny, Mother. Drive."

"Yes, ma'am."

Ten minutes later the two of them pulled up to the curb.

"Wow," her mother breathed.

"What's wrong?"

"This place looks like something out of a science fiction film."

Eleanor grimaced. "Somehow, I would have expected that from Victor Russo."

"He's a stuntman like Jack?"

"Yes, but with a taste for loud parties and even brasher women."

"It figures."

With Regina's help, Eleanor made her way to the third-floor apartment and pounded on the door.

"Maybe he isn't home," Regina suggested after several moments.

"He *has* to be home," Eleanor insisted determinedly, thumping on the panels again. "Victor!"

Distantly she heard the squeak of floorboards, a pause, then the rattle of a chain.

"Eleanor?" Victor's voice sounded gruff and sleep laden.

"Has Jack gone to Los Angeles?"

"How the hell should I know? I haven't seen him...since the...show."

"Do you have his home address in L.A.?"

"Sure." His voice was confused and slurred—as if he were hung over—or worse yet, drunk. "But he's not there. He's working on a project in San Francisco."

"I need the address."

"I...don't know," he said reluctantly. "Jack doesn't like women around when he works, it—"

Eleanor heard her mother take a step forward, then an "oof!" from Victor as if she'd poked him in the stomach.

"Listen up, buster. I'm this girl's mother and her son's grandmother and they both need to get in touch with Jack. *Now.* Either you can cooperate or I can get you *really* drunk, dress you in lingerie, take pictures and send them out as Christmas cards."

"Mother."

Regina gripped her elbow. "Quiet," she hissed. "He's gone to get the information."

"You're incorrigible," Eleanor muttered.

"Not at all. I'm a woman who knows what she wants. Just like my daughter."

WITHIN THE HOUR Regina was pulling up to the loading zone at the airport.

"Are you sure you don't want me to go with you?" Regina asked with obvious trepidation. "I could take care of the baby."

Eleanor leaned over to kiss her cheek. "You've

got to get back to the store. A sky cap will show me to my gate.'' She smiled, hitching Eric's infant seat more tightly into the crook of her arm. ''As for this little one,'' she said caressing the fuzz on his head with a maternal finger, ''he's never any trouble, and you know it. Besides, I've learned it isn't a crime to ask for help if I need it.''

Her mother squeezed her shoulder. ''Go on,'' she said huskily. ''And call me as soon as you're in San Francisco.''

Eleanor waved to show she'd heard. Then when a sky cap approached her, she said, ''I've only got the one bag and a diaper bag, but I'll need some assistance getting to my gate. I'm not very familiar with the airport.''

''Yes, ma'am.''

Taking the gentleman's arm, she strode into the terminal.

The trip to San Francisco was comparatively short, but to Eleanor, the minutes ticked past with frustrating slowness. She passed the time by stroking Eric's cheek as the engines lulled him to sleep and rehearsing what she would say to Jack when she saw him. When the flight attendant instructed the passengers to prepare for landing, Eleanor could have whooped in relief.

But she didn't whoop. Instead, asking the stewardess to radio ahead, she was met at the gate by another sky cap who took her directly to a waiting taxi.

''Where to?'' the cabby asked.

''There's a movie being shot on Pier Six.''

"Yeah, there, is," he stated wearily. "But they won't let you anywhere near it. I've had three passengers today try the same routine."

She offered him what she hoped was a mysterious smile. "I'm with the stunt crew."

"Oh, really?" he asked, clearly skeptical. "Doin' what?"

She shrugged. "A little of this, a little of that."

"Uh huh." It was clear that he didn't know whether to believe her or not, but after a moment's silence, she heard the click of the meter. Then he stomped on the gas pedal.

As they hurtled through the maze of airport traffic and began heading toward Pier Six, Eleanor found herself clutching Eric's infant seat more protectively against her hip and crossing her fingers in a childish wish.

Just let me on the set. Just let me talk to Jack.

The cab screeched to a halt.

"We're here, lady."

"Thank you."

She paid for her fare, adding a good-sized tip.

"Hey, thanks!" the man said as he helped her alight and handed her the bags she'd brought with her from Denver. "I'll just take you over to that guy holding a clipboard. He looks like he's part of the crew. Then I'll stay put until I'm sure somebody's taken care of you, okay?"

She smiled. "Thanks. I appreciate that." Around her, she could hear the shouts of various voices and the roar of what sounded like boat motors.

The cabbie walked her closer to the noises, pausing only once to help her duck under a string of plastic cordon tape.

"Here's the man with the clipboard," the cabbie muttered under his breath.

"Sir, I wondered if you could—"

"Eleanor!"

She frowned, not recognizing the voice.

"One-Eye?"

"Sure! How are you?"

She wilted in relief. "Fine, now."

"What are you doing here?" One-Eye asked. "I thought you were still in Denver?"

"I need to talk to Jack. Is he here?"

One-Eye chuckled. "Yes, ma'am. And I couldn't be a happier man to see *you* here, as well. He's been grouchier than a bear with a sore paw. But you'll have to wait for him to come down."

"Come down?" the cabbie asked before Eleanor could do so.

"He's up there."

"Where?" Eleanor asked.

"On top of the warehouse. He's got to fall four stories onto an air mat."

Four stories onto an air mat.

Eleanor's stomach immediately tightened, and every fear she'd ever experienced concerning Jack's job rushed over her like a scalding tide.

"How long until he...comes down?"

"Any minute. But he's an old woman where safety is concerned, so he won't jump until he knows the preparations are just right. He's always been a stickler for details, but since he met you he's especially careful.''

Careful.

The word stuck in her brain. Careful. Jack had always been careful. How many times had Jack told her the same thing? He'd insisted that he took every possible safety precaution, but a tiny corner of her brain had often wondered if he said that for her benefit alone. But now she was receiving the same information from One-Eye.

''He's good at what he does, isn't he?'' she said slowly, some of her unease draining away.

''He—heck, yes. He's the best. That's why they call him the Jack Man. Everyone in the business fights to be on his crew because they know he won't compromise on preparations.''

He won't compromise.

Didn't she already know that about Jack? That he did everything wholeheartedly? It was that portion of his personality that had convinced him to take her skydiving, to introduce her to sculpting. It was that portion of his personality that made her feel loved, body and soul. She trusted him with her heart, her son, and her life. Wasn't it time to trust him with his own safety, as well?

Yes.

Yes.

The warm sun beat down on her head, melting the last shred of resistance away and leaving her feeling completely liberated. She loved this man so much, trusted him so much, it was time he knew her feelings himself.

She grinned at One-Eye asking, "Is there any way you can let him know that I'm here?"

"I can do better than that." His voice dropped. "Carl, put Jack on the headset."

She heard a tinny reply and realized that One-Eye must be wearing some sort of communication gear.

"I don't care if he's meditating. Tell him to save it for the Dali Lama. He's got a visitor."

Another silence.

"They're going to get him," One-Eye said.

"What did you mean by 'meditating.'"

"Sometimes he takes a minute to collect himself, gather his wits. It's just his way."

"Maybe I shouldn't disturb him."

One-Eye chortled. "I think he'll be a lot less *disturbed* if he knows you're here. Then, I'll—" He broke off, obviously listening to a voice in his earpiece. "Yeah? Jack, hold on. There's someone here who needs to talk to you."

Eleanor felt One-Eye placing the headset over her ears and positioning the tiny arm of the microphone in front of her mouth. She blushed when she caught the tail end of Jack's tirade.

"...told you not to bother me again until we get this damn shot, One-Eye."

"This isn't One-Eye," Eleanor said softly.

A dead silence met her ears.

"Hello?" she called.

"Eleanor?"

"Yes."

"What are you doing here?"

"Where else would I be?"

Another long pause.

"You must think I'm a louse."

"Why?"

"Because I left like that."

"Like what?"

He sighed. "I should have at least said goodbye. You should have been given a chance to yell at me."

"What for?"

"Listen, I know you're mad as hell...and frankly, I deserve it, but—"

"I'm not mad," she said calmly. "Granted, you've given me some trouble in tracking you down, but I've found you now."

"Eleanor? What are you saying?"

She heard the tense quality of his voice. The time for blatant honesty had come.

"You misunderstood my reaction at the gallery, Jack. I wasn't angry with you—I was *never* angry with you."

"But I didn't tell you—"

"Victor might have spilled the beans, but I'm sure you meant to talk to me about the accident once we returned to my apartment. You said you had something to tell me on several occasions, but we were always...distracted by other things. Am I correct in assuming that you meant to inform me of your presence at the accident?"

There was a long pause, then, "Yes. But I should have confessed to you much sooner."

"I'm glad you didn't."

"What?"

"I'm glad you didn't," she repeated more slowly and distinctly. "You see, I used to think about the man who helped me that night. Sometimes I used to dream about his face. I think I had something of a crush on him."

"You did?"

"Yes. He was very kind. He helped me through the trauma of my injuries and losing my sight. Every now and again I would wonder where he was, who he was. If you'd admitted you were that man, I might not have trusted my feelings for you as completely as I do now."

There was no reply, and she added, "I love you, Jack. If you'll take a stubborn, pigheaded, likes-to-go-skydiving sculptor as your wife, I'm accepting your proposal."

There was a sniff, then Jack's voice demanding, "Who the hell is listening in on this conversation?"

"Me," a woman's voice admitted.

"Me too," a gruff man confessed.

"Count me in."

"I caught most of it."

"Could you go back to that part about—"

"Enough!" Jack shouted, then, "Eleanor, hang on. I'll be right down."

"I'm not going anywhere," she said softly. Then she removed the headset and gave it back to One-Eye.

"I'm the one who brought her from the airport," the cabbie informed anyone who would listen.

Within seconds Eleanor felt the energy level of the people around her soar.

"Roll cameras!" someone shouted from several yards away.

An expectant hush settled over the onlookers, and Eleanor looked up, up. The sun was bright and hot, allowing her to see the faintest shades of gray against a field of black. Then, just as the crowd offered a whispered oh-h, she thought she saw—or maybe imagined—a speck of a shadow plummeting down from above. Then there was a giant whoosh of air.

"He's down," One-Eye announced proudly.

Within seconds Eleanor heard the impatient footsteps striding toward her. Then the infant seat was taken from her hands, and she was scooped against Jack's chest.

"I love you," he whispered next to her ear. "You and Eric both."

"I know."

"I don't ever want to lose either of you again."

"You never lost us the first time."

His thumb tilted her chin, and his lips closed over hers for a passionate kiss.

Around them there was a sputter of applause, then the shuffle of onlookers returning to their work.

Jack lifted his head, calling out, "Do you need a retake?"

"I think that'll do it."

"Good. If you need me, I'll be at my hotel. One-Eye, you're in charge."

"Okeydoke."

Jack wrapped his arm around her waist. "Hey, cabbie. Are you free?"

"Yes, sir."

"Then take us to the Hilton."

"Yes, sir!"

The driver's feet scrabbled against the pavement as he hurried back to his car.

Eleanor laughed. "You're a lucky man. A successful jump, an empty cab…"

"Enough with the small stuff. Right now we have a wedding to plan. Then, later tonight, I'll see what I can do about introducing you to a friend of mine who has a cameo appearance in this project."

"What friend?"

"Bob Redford."

Eleanor halted in surprise, her mouth dropping.

Jack chuckled, touching her chin to close her jaw. "After that, we'll check out the flights to Alaska."

"Alaska?" she breathed in disbelief.

"It's the last of your wishes."

"What wishes?"

"Skydiving, Robert Redford and making love under the aurora borealis. You're on your own with the art show."

Vaguely she remembered that afternoon in The Flick when she'd railed at Jack about all of the dreams she'd lost. Little had she known that she'd never really lost them. They'd merely been hidden from view. This man had shown her how to find them. Because of him she had been drawn out of the shadows and into the light.

And at the moment there was no place on earth she would rather be.

Epilogue

Eleanor Rappaport MacAllister quietly closed the door to the adjoining hotel room and padded into the master suite she was sharing with her husband.

Husband. She doubted that she would ever grow tired of the term. She and Jack had been married for more than two years, yet she still felt as much the newlywed as she had during their long-delayed honeymoon to Alaska. Even now she could clearly remember the cool bite of the evening as Jack had pulled aside their rented Range Rover so that she could watch the swirling lights of the aurora borealis. It had been mere weeks after her second transplant surgery, and the colors had been so real, so vibrant, so beautiful, that she'd spent a good portion of the evening crying at the sheer beauty of the moment.

She still wondered how she could have been so blessed to find such a man. Jack was everything she had ever wanted in a husband and more. He was attentive, devoted—and still completely head over heels in love with her. He was a wonderful father to Eric. He supported her in her work and her aspirations.

But more than that, he'd made so many of her dreams come true—dreams she hadn't even known she was secretly harboring in her heart.

A pair of strong arms circled her from behind.

"Happy?" Jack murmured against her cheek.

"Deliriously so."

"And you should be. Imagine being a sculptor of so little experience and being asked to exhibit your work at a special showing at the Louvre."

Her laughter was low and triumphant.

"And here I thought I'd be the one to fulfill the last of your wishes."

She walked with him to the open windows and stared out at the indigo sky, the glittering city lights of Paris, and in the center of it all, the gleaming structure of the Eiffel Tower.

"It's beautiful," she breathed.

He held her close, whispering gruffly. "And I'm so glad that you can see it, actually *see* it."

She clung to him, her gratitude profound and immeasurable. After suffering the loss of her sight, she had thought that life held nothing but uncertainty. But with this man's help, she'd discovered the joys that awaited her, whether or not her surgery was successful.

"So you don't mind the glasses," she asked. Although her vision was nearly perfect, she still needed a slight correction in her left eye.

"I think they make you look sexy." Jack's hand

slid low over the silk of her nightgown. "But then, I think you look sexy in just about anything."

She turned in his arms. "Eric is asleep in the next room," she said enticingly.

His hands began to skim over her body in wonderful ways.

"Perfect."

"Room service brought up wine and cheeses," she said, then gasped when he nipped at a sensitive spot on her neck.

Jack took her hand, resolutely drawing her in the direction of the bed.

"Later. Right now you're all I need, Eleanor Rappaport MacAllister. You're all I've ever needed to make my life complete."

And as she sank beside him on the feather bed, Eleanor couldn't help but whisper, "As are you, my darling. As are you."

Visit us at www.eHarlequin.com

CNM0700

Coming this September from

You met the citizens of Cactus, Texas, in
4 Tots for 4 Texans when some matchmaking
friends decided they needed to get
the local boys hitched!

And the fun continues in

BY

JUDY
CHRISTENBERRY

Don't miss...
THE $10,000,000 TEXAS WEDDING
September 2000
HAR #842

In order to claim his $10,000,000 inheritance,
Gabe Dawson had to find a groom for Katherine Peters
or else walk her down the aisle himself. But when he
tried to find the perfect man for the job, the list of
candidates narrowed down to one man—*him!*

Available at your favorite retail outlet.

HARLEQUIN®
Makes any time special ™

Visit us at www.eHarlequin.com

HARTOS2

Daddy's little girl... **THAT'S MY BABY!** by

Vicki Lewis Thompson

Nat Grady is finally home—older and wiser. When the woman he'd loved had hinted at commitment, Nat had run far and fast. But now he knows he can't live without her. But Jessica's nowhere to be found.

Jessica Franklin is living a nightmare. She'd thought things were rough when the man she loved ran out on her, leaving her to give birth to their child alone. But when she realizes she has a stalker on her trail, she has to run—and the only man who can help her is Nat Grady.

THAT'S MY BABY!

On sale September 2000 at your favorite retail outlet.

HARLEQUIN®
Makes any time special ™

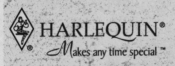